a BARTENDER'S *Holiday*

a BARTENDER'S *Holiday*

CAROLE LOVE FORBES

A Bartender's Holiday

Copyright © 2023 by Carole Love Forbes/Gary Love. All rights reserved.

No part of this publication may be reproduced, stored in a retrieval system or transmitted in any way by any means, electronic, mechanical, photocopy, recording or otherwise without the prior permission of the author except as provided by USA copyright law.

Published in the United States of America

ISBN 978-1-68486-394-5 (Paperback)
ISBN 978-1-68486-396-9 (Digital)

10.03.23

Contents

Chapter One 7
Chapter Two 13
Chapter Three 18
Chapter Four 30
Chapter Five 38
Chapter Six 43
Chapter Seven 47
Chapter Eight 52
Chapter Nine 61
Chapter Ten 69
Chapter Eleven 81
Chapter Twelve 90
Chapter Thirteen 103
Chapter Fourteen 109
Chapter Fifteen 117
Chapter Sixteen 130
Epilogue 137

CHAPTER One

Mac listened to the drunk automatically, with his ears, while his brain was going over the same familiar ground, bringing back that old nagging longing which left him aching on the inside.

How does a man miss the boat in his life? How does the guy voted Most Likely To Succeed in college wind up at age 38 behind a bar, listening to other people's bellyaches—living his own dull life by acting as an amateur psychologist to every slob off the street for the price of a drink?

True, the bar was his. He owned it. He had bought it with the money he had saved during his tour in Nam, added to his mustering-out pay. It was money he had saved to start his married life.

He was aware that his face was smiling—his head nodding automatically. But his mind was back fifteen years earlier. His eyes had the haunted look which they always had when he thought of Ellen.

What had happened there? What had spoiled that typical all-American romance? Ellen Billings, his college sweetheart, the most popular girl on the campus, cheerleader for the football team, homecoming Queen, <u>had</u> waited for him. It wasn't a very unusual story—the college football hero going off to war—his tearful sweetheart seeing him off, vowing her undying love. And he had been one of the lucky ones. She had kept her promise, had waited, written wonderful, encouraging letters, made plans with him for their future. They both waited and prayed for the day they would be together again.

But when that day came, they realized that they had both changed too much. They tried to make their dream come true, but could not. It just hadn't jelled.

At first, in the glow of his homecoming, they had been on cloud nine. The sexual part was super, but they could no longer talk—or communicate. They had nothing in common any longer. He just couldn't get into the swing of her kind of social life. Stacy Vandermeyer's garden parties were not able to erase the memories of too many weeks and months of hell and misery—the futilities of war, the intimacy with death.

Those cocktail parties, with their stuffed shirt executives getting drunk and solving the world's problems, those rich and boring society matrons, and worst of all, the loving little wifeys who propositioned Mac behind the fern planters, or on the dance floor, had made him ready to throw up. It all had sickened him from the gut out.

So, he and Ellen had finally agreed to call it quits. With an empty feeling inside, he had jumped on the first plane out of Los Angeles heading for the Big Apple, New York City. Well, what now? There he stood in Manhattan, the city of dreams, feeling heartbroken and frustrated too. He was still young, alive, and well; and he wanted to do something big with his life.

After all, wasn't he a golden boy—didn't everyone say he was going to be really BIG and RICH someday?

After a couple of weeks just wandering around New York, drinking in the excitement and pace of the city, he set out to get that "special" job that would start him on his way to his first million. After all, wasn't that "the American dream"? He wound up as a junior account executive at a leading advertising agency on Madison Avenue.

With his dark good looks, his 6'4" athletic body and his Irish charm, he had been an instant success. Three years later, he was a vice president with a salary to match—and he was thoroughly fed up! The rat race had finally got to him. He just got up one morning, feeling a little more frustrated and useless than usual, and said, "To hell with it!" He realized that he still valued his sanity, so...exit the advertising business!

What next?! He still had most of his Viet Nam savings, plus most of what he had earned in advertising. Hell, he hadn't had time to spend it. The only social life he had had was spent lining up clients—wining and dining bores of all descriptions—on the company expense account. His own money languished in several bank accounts—and grew fatter. It was now burning a hole in his bank book.

If anyone were to ask him why he finally settled on becoming the proud owner of a cocktail bar, Mac would have been at a total loss to answer. It had just been there—available, and he had just been there, also available, so.... All he knew was that a month later, he was the owner of "Delaney's Bar and Grill," which he promptly changed to "Mac's Haven".

It had been exciting at first, learning a totally new business, being his own boss, fixing up the bar, getting acquainted. He had felt a sense of belonging, of doing something interesting for the first time since the war.

That soon wore off though, and routine settled in. Oh, it wasn't a bad life, if you didn't mind the boredom. The demands were few; a couple of nights a week behind the bar, an automatic charm, and you had it made. It provided a little more than adequate income, and aside from the built-in social work with his customers, his life was pretty unencumbered.

"Only," he wondered, "where does the living come in? When do you do something that is motivated? When do you start to feel?" And, that most nagging question of all, "Where did love go?" He agonized, "Is there no second chance—no reprieve? Hell, even the most hardened criminal could look forward to a new chance—to be let out on bail, on parole." His mind was once again trapped in the familiar vicious circle—the maze which seemingly had no exit. He felt the frustration rise up from his gut into his throat, strangling him with its intensity.

"And Gladys said she'd stay at her mother's this time, if I didn't immediately mend my ways." A familiar voice penetrated Mac's brain and brought him back again to the present. "I told you last time she left me, she stayed away six whole months, didn't I?"

Mac slowly forced his attention back to the inebriate, arry Harlacher, who was at the moment, holding the floor at the bar. It was early, but then Harlacher was no respecter of hours. Any hour of the daily 24 might find him at one bar or another.

"Yeah, you told me," Mac managed.

"She just can't seem to understand that a guy needs a little freedom. When a guy works as hard as I do, he deserves a little liquid refreshment now and again," Harlacher managed to enunciate. "Don't you agree, Mac?…Dontcha?" Harlacher rubbed his very bald head with a thin, long-fingered hand.

"Well," Mac hedged. "I guess she cares about you and wants to see you stay sober; you can't blame her too much for wanting to be with you once in a while, can you?"

Harlacher strained his reddened eyes to focus on Mac's face. "You sidin' with her, Mac? Against me?!"

"Hell, no, Harry! You know me better than that. You're one of my best customers. I'm only trying to help you figure this mess out. I know you don't want to lose Gladys again, now do you?" he placated, while he mentally gritted his teeth.

"You're right, Mac," Harry replied, tears starting at the corners of his eyes. "You always been a good buddy to me, Mac. I ain't got no complaints. None at all." Harlacher pushed his glass toward Mac for a refill. "Don't pay me no mind, pal. I'm just goin' crazy with the thought of losin' my woman. We been married 42 years, Mac. 42 years!"

"That's a long time, Harry, and you aren't going to lose her," Mac assured. "Hey, I got an idea. Why don't you get her some flowers or candy, or something? That always does the trick! If you leave right now, you can just get to the florist on 98th street before it closes."

Harry brightened. "Hey, Mac. That's a swell idea. Knew I could count on you. I'll do it…right after I finish this drink."

Three hours later, Harry Harlacher was still finishing his drink when Paul Slater came in to relieve Mac. Mac had hired Paul three months before so he could have a few nights to himself. If he was going to do something about his life, he couldn't spend 24 hours a day of it behind a bar. He figured he might go to some dances, some social events—see if he couldn't find himself a nice woman.

"Hell, there must be some woman out there who could go for a guy like me," Mac thought. Mac was handsome, in a rugged, angular way. He had the strong jaw, the stubborn chin of his Irish ancestors, and his hair was thick and black, with just a touch of grey coming in at the temples—which only added to his masculine appeal. The serious blue eyes were fringed with short, thick black lashes that made his eyes stand out against the deep tan he had picked up during weekend afternoons at Far Rockaway. The beach was about his only form of recreation, except for his three mornings a week at the local gym, which kept him in vital good health and energy. It invigorated him, but somehow it seemed to make the dullness of his life more unbearable.

Sure, there were plenty of women handy to relieve him physically. In spite of his best efforts, the bar was usually crawling with call girls, plus a generous sprinkling of frustrated housewives looking for a fling. But that was not what Mac was looking for. If that was not enough, there were always places where a man could "purchase" a little diversion. Mac had tried it, but for some reason it had turned his stomach. Besides, with his looks and his virile, 6'4" frame—plus his ample manhood, Mac didn't have to "pay" for his diversions.

He had taken full advantage of all of this when he had first started his business, but now he found it no longer satisfied him. He was tired to death of quick, meaningless sex. He wanted a sincere relationship with a decent woman—like Ellen. Sometimes he still wished they could have made it, but…

So, he had hired Paul, who was a nice, companionable guy and a good bartender, and went out to investigate New York nightlife. He had gone to a few disco joints and only ended up feeling more "out of it" than ever. He was old enough to remember dancing with a girl in his arms. Then dancing had been a subtle way of making love. This crazy 'solo' sex-orgy dancing was definitely not his bag. Besides, most of the chicks were too young, and far too flamboyant for his tastes. The 'free love' Hippy types were more than he felt he could—or wanted to—handle.

Mac hung up his apron and briefed Paul for the night's work. Another night of free time and…well, he was getting a lot more reading in. Perhaps he'd take in another movie. "What is on TV tonight? Anything good?" he wondered. TV, that innocent-looking little box that lulled you into being satisfied with vicarious living—that King of all tranquilizers!

"Oh, well," thought Mac, as he slipped into his jacket, "50 million people can't be wrong. A color TV, a warm apartment, a fridge full of TV dinners and beer should satisfy you."

And, that other feeling? The urge to get out of the rut? That awful longing to 'do something worthwhile'—that was just the Devil stealing the peace and contentment out of his life. He had subjugated the longings pretty well so far. He could keep on doing so…couldn't he?

CHAPTER

Two

Mac said his automatic 'good nights' to Paul and Joyce, his cocktail waitress, pulled his coat's collar up around his chin, shoved his hands into his pockets, and pushed his way out the door. The night air, though brisk, felt good on his face again—too good to go immediately to his stuffy 5th floor walk-up, where all the heat of the day accumulated.

He decided to walk. Just walk—he didn't know or care where. He just knew that the feeling of frustration was stronger tonight than usual. He felt jumpy inside—sort of itchy—almost as if in anticipation. But that was silly. What reason could he have for feeling that way? It was just another night—just another midnight walk.

A half hour later, he came out of his reveries to find himself on 59th Street, near the park. He'd always loved Central Park. It was a little oasis in the middle of that big, steel and concrete jungle. The trees looked so strong and picturesque against the moonlit sky—like black lace on a silvery background.

"It's a damned shame," he thought. "You should be able to walk in the park at night and enjoy it. This damned city, with its one criminal for every three victims! It's sure no place to live." He wondered why he stayed here. Why hadn't he sold out and left this "summer festival" long ago?

On the other hand, where was there to go? At least the city was alive…even if he wasn't. He knew he couldn't stomach the hypocrisy of a small town, like the one in Ohio that he'd grown up in. And the other big cities? Los Angeles? Chicago? How much different were they, really? They all had their crime, their dopers, the ethnic battles, the gay element.

"Awe, hell, what the shit!" thought Mac. "I'm open minded. 'Live and let live', and all those old clichés." Anyway, Manhattan was his home now for better or for worse. If the City could put up with MacDonald Patrick Neely, he could put up with the City.

Without realizing it, he had slowed to a stop, and was just standing there in the shadows gazing meditatively at the outline of the park against the sky—when it happened!

He felt himself being spun around as something, or someone, flashed by on his right side. It had happened so fast that by the time he caught his balance, he was just barely in time to see the figure of a woman illuminated momentarily by the streetlight, disappear around the corner of a building into the alley, about 25 feet ahead of him.

Fortunately, as he had been spun around, he had also been flattened against the wall, because at that moment, a large man rushed by him, and due to the deep shadows, missed seeing Mac standing there—open mouthed. Mac's surprise left him momentarily immobilized. As he stood, stunned, with his back to the wall, he thought he heard the muffled sound of a scream coming from the alley ahead of him. He could also make out the sounds of a struggle.

What should he do? He looked up and down the street quickly in search of a policeman—or anyone—who might be called to help. The streets were empty. When was a New York street ever empty?!

He instinctively moved toward the alley but stopped as he got a few feet inside. He had better not get involved. Then again, a woman was in trouble, and he was the only one who knew about it. It seemed like he considered for a long time; but it was really only an instant. The sounds of the struggle continued unabated.

In the end, it was his body that made the decision. He found himself moving forward quickly but stealthily—his old army instincts

reawakened. A moment later, he was swallowed up in the darkness of the alley, with his arms hooked tightly around the throat of the man he had followed. The man was even bigger than Mac had estimated in the few seconds he had seen him in the light. And, he was strong! Mac was grateful for the hours spent at the gym on 57th street. They grappled silently but fiercely, each sustaining stinging blows, Mac wishing there was some light. As Mac struggled against the big man, his eyes gradually became accustomed to the darkness.

He caught his breath as he spotted the gun as it came out of his opponent's pocket. He grabbed for the man's wrist. He thought his arm muscles would burst apart from the pressure as he pushed the heavy muscular arm away from his body, struggling with the last of his energies now that it was a fight for his life. Fear and anger blended to give him added strength.

Mac breathed a sigh of relief as he heard the gun hit the ground near them. His relief was short-lived though, because this giant of a man, in his desperation, had also put on an extra burst of strength. All of Mac's resources went into holding his own with this man who fought like a veritable Hercules.

Mac stifled a cry of pain as his head hit the wall when he was thrown against an adjacent building. He experienced a feeling of hopeless despair, as his mind reeled, and he fought for consciousness.

The dizziness disappeared instantly as he was harshly pulled back to lucidity by the sharp sound of a shot ringing out, piercing the stillness of the late hour. He held his breath and waited for the pain to start, and the numbness that he heard preceded death—if death was not instantaneous.

It didn't come! Finally, it dawned on him that he was not hit. His brain at last totally clear, he realized that his eyes were now functioning quite well in the semi-darkness of the alley. The first thing he spotted was the huddled form of the big man, sprawled in the middle of the alley. Confusion set in for a moment; until he noticed the seated form of a woman behind the big man's hulk.

He moved cautiously toward the pair, and as he got near the woman, he could see she was still holding the gun in her two hands, which now rested slackly in her lap. Tears were streaming down her face, white streaks against her dust-covered cheeks.

He moved toward her quickly, knowing it would be no time at all before the alley was swarming with cops. That shot would bring them on the double.

He spoke softly. "Lady…lady. We've got to get out of here, fast!" She continued to stare at the body of the big man in shocked horror. He knew he would get no cooperation from her in the state she was in, so he quickly bent down, took the gun and pocketed it, then picked her up and fled along the alley in the opposite direction from where they had all entered. It seemed like hours ago, but it was actually only a matter of minutes.

In spite of his haste, he noticed how light this mystery was. Even though she had fainted and was dead weight, he guessed she couldn't weigh much more than a 12-year-old girl.

As he burst, breathlessly, out onto the street at the far end of the alley, he could hear the police sirens merging on the spot from several directions.

He really panicked then, for the first time. What the hell was he doing standing here on the street in the middle of the night, holding a murderess in his arms? What was he going to do with her? He couldn't very well just walk down the street with a woman dangling from his arms. It would be, to say the least, a bit suspicious.

His mind stood still for a second. Then, thank God, his instincts took over again. He adjusted the woman's body in his arms and lifted her over one shoulder, thus gaining a free hand. Then he ran quickly across the street to the nearest cars that were parked there. He systematically tried the doors. Number seven opened easily to his touch, and he sighed with relief as he dumped the woman onto the front seat and jumped in behind the wheel.

He had just time enough to arrange her so that she sat propped up against his shoulder, when two policemen came flying out of the alley. They split up, and Mac felt he was home free as the cop who headed his way ran past, gun in hand, looking cautiously around him. Mac caught his breath as the cop stopped a few feet past the car, turned around, and headed back towards him.

Mac quickly bent his head and engulfed the woman in his arms, as if he were engrossed in lovemaking. He prayed silently, but fervently. As prepared as he was for anything, he couldn't help jumping as he heard the tap of the cop's nightstick on the car window. His heart was beating so hard, he could hardly breathe.

He took a deep breath and, keeping the woman's head nestled on his shoulder protectively, he looked up and saw the cop motioning him to open the window. With the ugly and dangerous-looking police revolver staring him in the face, he quickly complied—as quickly as his shaking hand would allow.

CHAPTER

Three

"Okay, fella, outa the car," the officer demanded. Mac figured that if his Madison Avenue charm had ever been needed, now was the time.

"What'sup, officer, sir?" he smiled innocently, adding just enough slur to his speech to suggest a few too many drinks.

"You are, if you don't get out of there—and fast," the cop growled. Then he noticed the woman for the first time, and added, "Someone in there with you?"

"Sure, off'cer. My girl. We was jus' doin' a little neckin' before we went home from the show."

"There's no theatre in this neighborhood," the policeman rasped.

"Course not, off'cer. But, it's darker and more private up here nere t'park." He winked, "Ya know whut I mean?" The cop just stared at him.

"The lady lives way out in Far Rockaway. We haven't made hay where we can yet," he said, adding a suggestive chuckle.

"What's the matter with her?" the officer growled, trying to get a better look into the car.

Mac cuddled her closer as he pretended to inspect her. "Looks like she passed out, off'cer. Well, how t'hell d'ya like that. We did have a

few drinks after t'theatre, but t'go and pass out on me…what the hell? Can ya beat that?"

The officer's partner ran up to the car at that moment out of breath and impatient.

"What we got here…anything?"

"Naw, just a couple of homeless neckers. You find anything?"

"Nothing up the other way. I'm afraid who ever it was got away. We'd better report back—pronto!"

The second cop turned to Mac. "You, Mac, did you see anyone run out of that alley just now?"

The use of his name startled Mac for a moment, but he realized it was just being used generically. Mac answered vaguely, "Alley? What alley?"

The first cop rallied. "Didn't you hear a shot just a few minutes ago?"

Mac considered seriously, but drunkenly, and finally replied. "Thought tha' wuz fireworks from kissin' this lil' gal here. You meanta tell me it wasn't? Hell, some disappointment!"

The officers looked at each other in disgust. "What'll we do with these two lovebirds?" the first cop asked. "The dame's passed out. Shall we throw them in the drunk tank and let 'em sleep it off?" Mac held his breath.

"No. No time to waste on them now. Let's go!" the second officer yelled as he started off, on the run, for the alley entrance.

The first cop looked a little reluctant to leave a situation that didn't quite smell right to him. But Mac grinned at him sheepishly and lisped, "Aw, com'mon off'cer. Have a heart. Ain't you never been in love?"

"Love," the officer grunted skeptically. "Okay, but move on. I don't want you hanging around here. There's been a shooting and it's not safe around here. Take your lady home to wherever you said she lived. We've got work to do."

For a second, Mac really panicked. His heart was pounding even louder than before, and he was afraid the perspiration forming on his forehead would be a dead giveaway. How could he take the officer's excellent advice and get away from there, when he was in a car that was not his? He felt, hopefully for the panel but as he feared, no key hung in the slot. He was trying to think of some excuse that wouldn't make the already suspicious cop even more suspicious when the officer growled at him.

"Uh, uh, Bud. You're not driving in that condition. You got any money?" Mac nodded assent. "Then you hop a cab. You can come back after your car tomorrow. And, don't let me catch you parking around here anymore. We got troubles enough without babysitting a couple of screwball lovebirds."

Mac tried not to show the great sense of relief that flooded over him as he opened the door. With the help of the impatient officer, he pulled the woman's still unconscious form out of the car and gathered her in his arms. The cop locked and slammed the car door and whistled down a passing cab. Mac staggered, he thought rather convincingly, under the weight of the woman as they tumbled into the cab.

"Thanks, off'cer," he offered effusively. "Really 'preciate it. Nice to know t'taxpayer's gettin' somethin' fer his money."

The cop scowled at him and slammed the cab door. Then he turned quickly away in answer to a shouted summons from his partner, who had come back to the entrance of the alley. The last Mac saw of him was his back, as he ran full tilt into the alley, on the heels of his partner.

For the first time in hours, it seemed, Mac could breathe freely. He leaned back against the seat of the cab and let the tension ooze out of his now aching body, as he took in great gulps of air.

"Where to, Mac?" the cabbie grumbled impatiently. "I ain't got all night! Gotta make a living, too."

"Hell," thought Mac. Did everyone in town know him by name? Oh, well, there was always 'George' and 'Bud.' They got their share, too.

"Hey, Mac! Wake up! Where yaw wanna go?"

Where to? Funny how two such simple little words could instigate such a major calamity. Where to? How the hell did he know!

He looked down at the girl in his lap, for he could see now in the light of the streetlamps, that she was just a girl, and it struck him again. What the hell was he, Mac Neely, doing here in a cab near Central Park at 1 o'clock in the morning with a strange girl unconscious on his lap, the police breathing down his neck, and a smartass New York cab driver yelling at him, "Where to?" Mac searched his mind. "Yeah, where the hell to?"

"Look, Mac, either tell me where you want to go or get the hell out'a my cab!"

"245 East 97th street," Mac heard his voice saying. Home was the only place that came to mind. The cab lurched into motion, and tore off down the street at such a pace that Mac was alarmed they might be stopped for a speeding ticket. That was all he needed at this point!

He adjusted the girl more comfortably in his lap, and wondered at the length of time she had been out. Maybe he would do better to take her to a hospital. For all he knew she might be wounded or have a concussion—anything. He tentatively checked her limbs to see if anything appeared to be broken. She had bruises on her arms, but they didn't appear to be too bad. He caught the eye of the cabbie in the windshield mirror, and was trying to think of some casual thing to say to allay suspicions, but being used to the life of a New York cab driver, he just shrugged and went back to the rigorous job of making his way through the heavy traffic.

"He's smart," thought Mac. "Don't get involved! That's the ticket in a place like New York—that is, if you want to survive."

Satisfied that there didn't seem to be any serious wounds, Mac rejected the hospital theory. He knew he would have a tough time explaining who she was and what had happened to her.

No, he'd better stick to his original course and take her to his apartment. He could patch her up with his first aid kit, and put her in a warm bed.

"It's probably shock more than anything else," he figured. And, if she didn't come out of it by morning, then he'd figure out how to get her some medical help.

"Poor little thing. She looks like a little kid sleeping peacefully after a hard day at school. Wonder who the hell she is and what she was doing in that alley?" His thoughts were rudely interrupted as the cab screeched to a hair-raising halt in front of his apartment house on East 97th. He paid the cabby, adding a very generous tip to keep him happy (if such a thing is possible for a man in his employ), and with some effort, pulled himself and the girl in his arms out of the cab and onto the curb. The cab tore away, and Mac glanced quickly up and down the street to see who was in evidence. There was only an old man down to his left about three-quarters of a block, busily preoccupied curbing his small dog.

Mac quickly ran up the brownstone steps, and fumbled in his pocket for his key, all the while trying to balance the girl's weight so he wouldn't drop her.

A few minutes later, he pushed open the door to his own small, but neat, apartment; then pushed it closed with his hip. With some effort he flicked the light switch on with his elbow and breathed a sigh of relief to find himself and his mysterious burden safely on home territory. He was breathing hard from the five flights of steps, not wanting to be too conspicuous in the rickety elevator. Its lack of efficiency making the building a walk-up.

He laid the girl carefully on the couch, glad of the relief on his sore arm muscles. His body was starting to ache all over now. In spite of his workouts at the gym, he hadn't had a real fight like that in years, and his body was screaming at him.

He set to work immediately at washing away the dust and perspiration from the girl's face and hands, though he was dying for a good strong drink. He loosened the collar of her blouse, and then inspected her once more for any head injuries or wounds to her body. Aside from quite a few bad bruises from her very one-sided struggle with their dead giant-sized friend, he could find no signs of serious injury. He wondered again at the length of time she had been unconscious. It didn't seem normal to him. He looked into her face searchingly, and once again noted how young and vulnerable she looked. She couldn't be over 20-21 years old. She was small and delicate of build, with black hair that fanned out on the pillow in great waves, and must, he figured, hang down to her waist. She wore her hair straight, and even with the dust of the alley in it, its gleam and silky texture could not be disguised. There was something about her features that puzzled him. Something different, a look he couldn't quite put his finger on.

Concerned she might wake up without him there, he took a very quick shower and washed the grime out of his hair. Feeling at least 85% better, he sat near the girl on the couch. Total exhaustion was now setting in, and from the feel of his muscles, he knew he would be sore for a couple of days.

He gathered what was left of his waning strength and lifted the girl gently and carried her to his bedroom. There, he deposited her carefully on the bed, and removed her shoes and hose. He decided he'd better take her blouse and skirt off too, if she was going to rest comfortably.

In spite of the condition he was in, his body felt a spark of desire as he looked at her in her panties and bra. Being tiny, she was not too huge in the breast department, but her breasts were in perfect proportion to her body, round and firm and coming to soft points at the tips, which was evident through the almost invisible, flesh-colored net bra she wore. He ventured that if he had a tape measure, he would find that she had the traditional hourglass figure of around 10 inches difference in the size of her waist to the bust and hips. Her body, even in its unconscious state, was graceful and feminine. His heart caught in his throat. "You are a dirty old man, Mac Neely," he thought to himself. "A lecher!" But, in spite of his self-censure, he had difficulty in taking his eyes off her young, fresh beauty. Her skin had an unusual glow to it that gave it a satiny look.

He finally forced himself to pull the sheet and a light blanket up over her, knowing that she should not get a chill in her condition.

"How did such a girl as this get mixed up with a big thug like that—and what was the connection? Had the guy just spotted her and decided to rape her? If so, then why the gun?" He was sure there was something more involved.

The question now was what to do with her. He knew that if she didn't regain consciousness by morning, he would have to assume it was something serious and get her to a hospital. It would be very sticky, but he couldn't just let her lay there and perhaps even die on him! The thought panicked him anew, and he gently pulled her arm from under the cover and felt for her pulse. He didn't know how to count it to see if it was normal, but he could feel it beating in what seemed to be a steady pattern, and she appeared to be breathing easily enough.

"Well, I'd better see what I've got left in the liquor cabinet," he said aloud. Being a man used to living alone, he often voiced his thoughts. It seemed to give him some kind of comfort to hear a human voice in that lonely apartment.

He rose with great effort and made his way to the living room, where he poured himself a good stiff shot of Bourbon and gulped it down greedily. He was amazed to find how much better he felt. He poured another, and after he had downed it, he caught himself going to sleep in the chair, and realized that if he didn't hit the sack soon, he'd never make it to the bed.

He slipped out of his robe—too tired to get the pajamas—and pulled down an extra blanket from the top of the closet. In order to be close to the girl, if she should regain consciousness, he laid down next to her on top of the covers, and before he was totally covered, he was enveloped in a deep, healing sleep.

He never knew what woke him. All of a sudden, he was just wide awake, staring into two bemused and frightened eyes. He sat up quickly, grabbing frantically at the blanket that had slipped off of him exposing his ample manhood. The girl was resting on one elbow, and when she saw his embarrassment, her natural youthful sense of humor got the best of her. The fear in her eyes was replaced by a twinkle, as she said in a voice that was soft, but clear, "Somehow you don't look too threatening sitting there holding that blanket up to you like a virgin on her wedding night." Her laugh tinkled out, and its quality was infectious. Mac found himself smiling, then they were both flat on their backs, weak and helpless with laughter.

The girl made no attempt to hide her body from Mac's gaze, as her lovely young breasts acted like a magnet to his eager eyes. As their laughter ebbed away, they found they were staring into each

other's eyes, both seeming to question the emotions that had begun to engulf them. The laughter had broken any barrier of strangeness between them.

Not even aware of how it happened, Mac found he was on top of her. Their lips met and clung, and his body felt the heat of her shapely body as a bonfire welled up from his groin to the top of his head.

His hand eagerly sought out the breasts that had captivated him since he first saw them. She must have unhooked the bra for him, because the flimsy garment came away quickly and easily. He fondled the delicious round firmness of her soft-tipped breast. He could feel the nipple erect as he caressed it—all the while continuing the kisses that set his head reeling.

She moaned softly as he let his hand travel down the soft curve of her young body until it reached the Mound of Venus, with its curling black hair. With her assistance, he slipped off her flimsy panties and entwined his fingers in the soft hair, savoring every moment of the experience. Not being able to resist, he transferred his kisses to one of her hard-tipped breasts, enjoying the firm warmth of it.

Not since Ellen had he felt his emotions respond so to the act of making love to a woman. This was somehow more than sex, it was living—feeling—wanting—needing, and (Oh, thank God) receiving! For the girl in his arms welcomed his caresses joyfully—fully—matching his ardor with her own.

In his joy, he almost couldn't credit that he was actually feeling her soft, young hand slip down and gently take hold of his manhood. He felt it jump with the ecstasy of her caresses. He moved his body around so that he could admire her womanhood, surrounded by the gleaming black mound of hair which glowed against her creamy, strangling glowing white skin. He couldn't believe the beauty of this passionate girl, as he lost himself in gazing at her loveliness.

She moved around, touching him everywhere as she moved. He felt the softness of her lips where he least expected them, and the excitement was so great that he could hardly contain himself. He pulled gently away to gather his senses, then returned the honor she had paid him. When he had brought her to the heights of ecstasy, he reveled in her joy. It thrilled him to see her react so to his lovemaking.

She moved around then, so that they could pleasure each other. The feeling she aroused in him nearly drove him out of his mind. He had to use every ounce of his strength to keep from reaching his completion prematurely. He knew a better place he wanted to fill with his manliness, and he knew he had better do it soon, or he wouldn't be able to contain the feelings that were battering away at him.

Gently, he moved around into a position to satisfy their deeper longings. His mind sought for words to describe how he felt at that instant. Somehow the old familiar four-letter words were not adequate or suitable for the experience he was having with this strange and beautiful girl.

His mouth sought hers desperately, as he gently, but firmly, plunged his manhood deep inside her. He nearly exploded at the mere entering, but he knew he had to hold on. He wanted this experience to be total, and for that, he must wait for her.

It was a blessing for him that she was as hot as he was, for in less than a minute, he felt her arch against him in a desire for fulfillment as great as his own. The heat from their bodies could have kept his apartment warm for a week.

He thrilled as her moans of pleasure grew and mounted until she practically screamed out her readiness. He was more than ready to complete her joy and his. He moved smoothly and surely, controlling his movements until the feelings exploded in him and he felt himself falling—down, down into a maddeningly passionate pit.

He knew not where he was. Somewhere in the middle of a black and red vortex, a kaleidoscope of joy, itch-like pain—spasm. He could hear what must be his voice somewhere off in the distance, making the strangled sounds of fulfillment. The climax was so long and profound that he could hardly believe it was happening to him. The aftershocks went on and on, until finally he lay totally exhausted and completely satisfied in her arms. Their bodies continued their gentle spasms for a minute or two, until…

In their mutual satisfaction and release, they fell into a deep sleep, still entwined in each others arms, his limp manhood still encased within her softness.

It was late in the afternoon when they awoke again, almost simultaneously. They grinned at each other in mutual understanding and happiness.

He could feel his manhood hardening within her, as in their deeply satisfying exhaustion, they had not moved since they dropped off to sleep. As he moved in an ever-increasing rhythm, he kissed her, and looking deep into her eyes, he was sure he saw the same depth of feeling there that he was feeling for her at that moment.

He smiled. "You know, we don't even know each other's names."

Her laughter tinkled out and she pulled him tight against her taut-tipped breasts. "Somehow, it doesn't seem to be too important, does it?" He kissed her again, and felt their bodies respond once more in a quick and stupendous climax which was even more earth-shattering than the previous one.

When they had both come down sufficiently to be able to function again, they lay pressed close together, his hand idly toying with her now soft breasts. She softly stroked his manhood in a way that gave him great pleasure, but not enough to make it come alive again too soon.

She nuzzled her face against his shoulder. "I guess the traditional question is, 'where am I?'"

"You're in the apartment of a strange, bedazzled man, whose life you saved—and who rescued you from a rather compromising and dangerous experience," he chuckled.

He was alarmed at her sudden stiffening. Her whole body went taut, and she pulled away from him and sat up in the bed. Suddenly all the wonderful warmth and intimacy was gone. She was a stranger once more—her eyes staring coldly ahead of her. He could almost smell the fear emanating from her.

He reached over and touched her arm tenderly and gently. She jumped, and looked down at him with a remote look in her almond shaped eyes—a blend of fear and questioning. It was as if she had just awakened for the first time—as if what had happened between them had never been.

He felt his heart sink! He knew somehow that no matter what, he did not want to lose this girl—he wanted the intimacy and the joy to return—he wanted her to look at him as she had when their bodies were joined in ecstasy, but he knew that he was once again a stranger to her.

"What is it?" he questioned. "What is this all about anyway? You can tell me. I don't know why, but I care about you—very much, and I want to help you." He pleaded.

It was a long time before she spoke, and when she did, she spoke softly, haltingly, as if she was being forced back into a world she didn't want to re-enter.

"There's nothing you can do. There's nothing anyone can do! Somehow, I'm here, and for the moment, safe—but, he'll get me.

When Kai wants someone dead, they're dead!"

"He won't be after anyone—ever again," Mac said quietly—to deaden the shock.

"You mean…?" Her eyes opened wide. "Oh, you mean the man in the alley? Oh, no. He's dead?" Mac nodded a silent, "Yes."

"God! Did I…did I…?" she stammered.

"Yes, but there was no other way. He was going to kill you. Besides, you're safe—now with him gone."

"No. No, unfortunately not. You see that was just one of Kai's henchmen. He's not important. My real enemy is much more formidable. He won't rest until I'm in my grave!" she sighed, a tear sliding down her cheek.

"Who?" Mac pressed. "Who is 'Kai' and why would he want you dead?"

She sat for a long time without moving. Then, as if she finally recognized something in him—perhaps the tone of his voice she turned and looked at him, searchingly. As she looked deep into his eyes, he could feel that she was beginning to remember who he was, and what they had shared. Finally, she spoke, haltingly at first, then more quickly, as if a dam which had long been welled up was beginning to crack.

"I don't know who you are, or why you brought me here, but I'm grateful—truly grateful. I remember last night now, as I begin to piece together a nightmare…I did kill him, didn't I?"

"As I said, I think so," Mac replied gently. "I must admit I didn't stay around long enough to make sure, but he sure looked dead. Why was he after you?"

She looked into his eyes as if to find the answer she was searching for, then made up her mind. "She's going to tell me everything," Mac acknowledged to himself. "That's good. It means she trusts me."

CHAPTER

Four

She spoke slowly...the emotion gone and only a deep sadness remaining in her voice. "It's not a new story. You hear it every day on television and movies—in magazine stories. The age-old story of a young girl letting her vanity and egotism ruin her life."

"I was sixteen when I met him. I was going to the International School in Bangkok. I'm Eurasian, you see. My mother was Thai and my father an American surveyor in the Far East on a work mission from the United Nations. Kai, that's his name," she shuddered. "Kai Ching was also Eurasian, and extremely handsome and charming. He was 25 at the time, and full of youthful strength and an unbounded ambition to become rich and powerful."

"The depth of his ambition frightened me at times, but in my inexperienced eyes, he could do no wrong. Even when I stumbled on the fact that he was getting involved in some really heavy things, I closed my eyes. I loved him, and I knew he loved me. My vanity blinded me to the fact that I might be just another tool for him to use—another rung on his ladder to success—and, as you know, rungs are made to be stepped on."

She sighed deeply. Mac kept his silence.

"I don't know how he got me started in the dope smuggling business. It was so subtle, so devious, and done with such charm, that

it was as natural as brushing my teeth in the morning. I knew in my heart that it was evil?" She looks at Mac questioningly.

"Mac," he said. "Short for Macdonald Patrick O'Neely."

"Mac," she continued. "Like I said, it's an old story. I 'm still vain enough, God help me, to hate most the fact that I was so stupid and gullible."

She looked at him, the pain evident in her eyes. "He had encouraged me to get the best education I could get in Bangkok, then to go to Hong Kong and enroll in Airline Stewardess training. At first, I was thrilled to think he was so ambitious for me, that he believed in me as a person, and wanted me to have a successful life, too."

"Of course, it was only to increase my usefulness to his 'business'."

She gazed meditatively into space. "It's funny how women can justify just about anything in the name of 'love'. As long as your man is pleased with you, you're happy. It doesn't seem to matter that what you are doing is wrong. You close your mind to the fact that you are helping to destroy the lives of thousands of people. I had to fight hardest not to think of the children, the young people whose lives would be over before they had even begun."

She turned to look at Mac again. "Opium is a horrible narcotic. One of the worst because it's so insidious. It's so subtle in its destruction of the human mind and body. It gets into your very fiber so that to think of giving it up would be like giving up the joy of sex, or food when you're starving."

Mac watched her closely, noting every change of expression on the lovely, wistful young face. The very lack of emotion in her voice somehow touched him more than if she had been in a state of hysteria. His heart felt a long-forgotten tug as he listened to her. Suddenly, she started to tremble. Mac took her in his arms. She was icy cold. The longer he held her, the worse she shook, and he felt the moisture from her tears falling onto his shoulder.

She pulled away suddenly, her face a tortured mask of what it had been just a few moments before. "I know, Mac," she cried out, "I know because he was smart enough to get me hooked on it, too. He had to have that last total control over me—something which to threaten me should my feelings toward him ever change."

With a sudden burst of energy, she leaped off the bed, and started searching the room frantically. "My purse! Mac! Where is it? You did get my purse, didn't you?!"

Spotting her clothes piled on a chair, she swooped down on them, tossing them this way and that in her frantic search, her young breasts bobbing freely as she moved.

"Where is it? Oh, God, where is it?!" she screamed. "I have to have it now!"

Mac jumped from the bed and, grabbing her, tried to calm her down. "Honey, stop...stop it! It's not here. The only thing I remember you holding was the gun. You must have dropped the purse in the struggle. Calm down!"

She stared at him for a moment in disbelief, then let out a heartrending wail, flaying at him with her small fists, her head tossing back and forth in her hysteria. "Stop, now. Stop. This isn't helping anything. Calm down," Mac begged.

She fought him hard, her sharp fingernails coming dangerously close to his face. In his desperation, he loosened his right hand from her shoulder and slapped her hard across the face. She let out one last scream as his hand hit, then went stiff in his arms, staring at him unseeingly. "It must be back there in the alley. I don't see any way we could get it now," Mac explained quietly. He felt her tremble all over, then her body went limp and she collapsed against him. He was afraid she had fainted, but she spoke again, in a strangled voice.

"Oh my God, Mac. Everything was in that purse. My opium, my paraphernalia...the...everything. Don't your see, I have to have it. The opium is wearing off.... I have to have some now! I just can't face life without it...please, Mac, please."

Mac held her close, somehow trying to make up for the needs she was feeling, but knowing there was only one thing that could help her at that moment. "Look, honey...oh, for God's sake, what's your name?!"

"Kim...Kim Henri," she replied, trying to control the shaking of her body. "Mac...what am I going to do?"

"I don't know, Kim. Let me think. I must know somebody who could get me some," he pondered.

"I know where to get it, but the minute I show up there, Kai and his thugs will be waiting for me," she sighed.

"This Kai, why is he after you? Why would he want to kill you?"

She was shivering so strongly now, that he led her back to the bed, grabbed a blanket and wrapped it tightly around her. Then he sat with her in his arms at the foot of the bed, and rocked her gently back and forth, as she, with great effort and through her tears, continued her story.

"I guess I had known for a long time that he really didn't love me, but I didn't want to believe it. To know that he was only using me was something I didn't want to admit to myself. It made a mockery of everything we had had together—made the smuggling I had done for him even more horrible—and somehow totally inexcusable. So...I kept lying to myself. I told myself that there were really no other women—that I was just being jealous and letting my imagination run away with me. All the while, I knew that when I was out of Bangkok on flights to London, Paris, or America—he was not spending his nights alone."

She took a deep breath, relaxing a tiny bit as she lost herself in her story. "There was something else, too.... Something...toward the end...something that he was into that is so horrible that he didn't even let me in on it. Something to do with...I think...the women he surrounded himself with."

She shivered violently. "Oh, Mac, I'm so cold. I have to have something now. I can't talk anymore."

"Yes, baby, you can...you can...just a little bit more. I have to know who and what I'm up against."

She looked up at him, her beautiful dark eyes pools of grief. She started again, struggling for every word. "I finally confronted Kai, and he just laughed at me. He told me I was being silly. He held me in his arms and kissed me and told me that I was his girl...his first and best girl, and that the others were merely poor copies of me. He said they were strictly business and didn't mean a thing to him."

"Foolishly enough, I fell for it. I was actually willing to live with that, until a few nights ago. I knew I didn't love him anymore, but I was in too deep. My mind had already sought every means of extricating myself from his clutches, but I was too firmly trapped…so…I knew I had to continue sleeping in the gutter-bed I had made for myself. It would have been easier, if we were still in Bangkok, but here, in New York, I know no one…I had no place to run to."

Mac pushed the hair back off her forehead, which was damp with perspiration. "You said, 'until a couple of nights ago.' What happened then to change it?…and who was that man in the alley?"

"That was Hermann, one of Kai's henchmen. He was sent to kill me—at Kai's orders, of course." She looked up at Mac, seeing the questions in his eyes. "Why? Because I had the temerity to refuse to become a whore for him…to act as a common come-on for Kai's little ventures into the Park Avenue circles."

"I had lost my airlines job when one of the girls reported that she suspected I was mixed up in something shady." She shivered again. "They couldn't come up with any proof…they had no actual evidence, but the suspicion was enough to get me fired. I was no longer paying my way, in Kai's opinion."

"He couldn't have me hanging around just living off him. His fantastic generosity to me just didn't quite extend that far. I had to pay my way, and the best way I could do that was to…to use all of the arts of "love" that he, himself had taught me."

Mac interrupted, "And taught you exceedingly well, I must say." He hugged her to him.

She managed a weak smile. "I couldn't do it, Mac. I just couldn't let myself sink any lower than I already was. I told him no. He was furious! He said I couldn't refuse. He said I had no mind of my own, and must do as he bid me. All of the worst of his Asian blood came out in him, and they can be viciously cold and heartless in dealing with anything or anyone who opposes them. The look in his eyes was

a death sentence, and I knew it. He had Kato, his other henchman, lock me in my bedroom."

"It took me most of the night, with having to be quiet and all, but I finally then got the window unlocked and got away down the fire escape."

Mac couldn't help but marvel at the strength she must have to carry out such an escape. He watched her face as she continued much more calmly now as he rocked her gently.

"I did okay the first day, but knew I had to have more opium than I had stuffed into my purse. The only way I knew to get it was through a dealer where I had made some deliveries. I knew it was taking a big chance, but I had no choice. I had already used up most of what I had, and I knew I couldn't face what was ahead of me without it." She stopped unable to continue. Mac stroked her hair gently.

"Go on, honey…go on…I have to know it all," he gently urged.

"I got the opium all right, but the dealer must have called Kai Ching. I had stopped in a doorway not far from the dealer and satisfied my needs…I wouldn't have made it much further if I hadn't, but I guess it gave Hermann just the time he needed to catch up with me. I ran! I don't know how far, but it must have been blocks…ducking in and out of doorways and cutting through hotel lobbies."

"I thought I had finally lost him, when he caught up with me near the park. Well, you know the rest." She looked up at Mac, and he was again struck by the beauty of those almond-shaped eyes. He knew now that it was the slight Asian look that had made her appear different to him when he had first studied her unconscious face in the taxi. Even in their present anguish, those eyes were something else! He felt something inside of him going soft, and he knew that whatever he had to do to help this strange young girl, he would do it.

Mac had been around dope and dealers enough during his stretch in Nam to know that he could handle himself all right on the street. Though he'd never gotten into the dope bag himself, he knew plenty of Nam vets who had. One, in particular, was a guy that he knew was still on the stuff and would know where to get what he needed.

"You'll have to clue me in on where not to go. Anyplace where Kai Ching is known would be too dangerous." Mac said.

"No," she cried. "I don't want you getting any more involved than you are. You don't know Kai! You don't…"

"Don't worry, I know what I'm doing. I have a few connections myself…" He stopped at Kim's startled look. "No, I don't indulge. Could never see any future in it. I just know someone who started using pot when he thought he didn't have a future…then he got onto the hard stuff. He's been able to point me in the right direction."

Kim lay quiet in his arms for the moment, the spasms in her body abating. He knew this calm wouldn't last too long, and that, for her sake, he must hurry. He found it difficult to move though, as he sat there gazing at the beautiful, helpless girl in his arms. He couldn't seem to concentrate on anything but those soft, pleading eyes and the delicate Eurasian features.

"There's just one thing I don't understand," he said, finally. "You just don't seem to be the kind of girl who would get mixed up with people like this. You're so…"

"Refined?" she finished for him. "Yes, Kai saw to that. He kept me sheltered from the lower elements in drug trafficking. My job, as you remember, and my education, were very respectable. I dealt only with the better class of clients, and even when I had to make a delivery in person, there were no words exchanged. Kai thought I would be more valuable to him that way."

Mac couldn't resist any longer. He gently pulled her toward him and put his lips to hers. Her lips were cold to the touch, and she was unresponsive at first, but slowly she thawed, and he felt his pulses leap as she started to respond to his kisses, letting her soft mouth open to his probing tongue, arching her small body so that her breasts, hardened now with desire, pushed against his chest. He could feel the life starting to flow into his member and threw himself into the kiss with all the fire that was starting to burn into his groin.

He heard a ringing sound somewhere in the distance. It seemed to be very insistent, and then Kim was pulling away from him, reluctantly, and he realized that it was his telephone ringing in the

front room. Funny, how strange the sound of the telephone bell seemed to him. It came as if from another world. A world that was forgotten, and somehow foreign to him now.

He gave Kim a swift kiss, and bundling the blanket tightly around her, laid her on the bed, and then went to answer the strange insistent instrument that continued to beckon him from that other world.

"Hello?" It was a girl's voice…Joyce's voice, from the bar, and it snapped him back into reality. He had forgotten completely about the bar…about Joyce, everything, in this strange thing that had so violently made its way into his life.

"Oh, Joyce. What time is it?" he asked, looking for his watch which he'd taken off and left on the bedside stand the night before. "Two o'clock! Oh, my God, honey. I'm sorry. Who's there? Well, you can't handle it all by yourself. Look, an emergency has come up, and I can't make it in today. Call Paul and see if he'll take over…yes, it might be for a night or two…no, I can't explain…not now. There's no time. Paul's number is on that card behind the cash register…and listen, Joyce, if he can't make it, give me a call back right away and I'll have to call an agency or something. Yes…I'll be leaving in about 15 minutes. That's right…if I don't hear from you in about 10 minutes, I'll assume everything's ok. Okay, baby?…Fine…and thanks, Joyce. You're a good girl. I'll see to it that you won't be sorry for being so reliable in a pinch. Okay, baby…Bye."

He replaced the receiver on the cradle slowly, shocked that he had so far forgotten his own life and his business in this involvement with a strange girl who had popped into his life so suddenly…and so violently.

He turned and rushed to the bedroom door, half expecting to see his old empty room. Perhaps it had all been a hallucination.

CHAPTER

Five

"Now, what made me say that? This is all so crazy," he thought to himself as he closed and locked the door of his apartment and started toward the rickety elevator. Taking his life in his hands, he entered the ancient elevator, wondering if it felt like working today or not... "There's no way I could be in love with someone I don't even know, and yet..."

Fortunately, today the elevator was on its best behavior and he stepped out into the lobby, if you could call a small entry way with a dilapidated old couch a lobby.

The street was, as usual, teeming with people of every shape, size, color, and demeanor. He loved the people of New York. They were a never-ending kaleidoscope of color, personality and activity. If one can learn not to hit back, and ignore getting snarled at, one can live very pleasantly in the Big Apple. There were times Mac found it very difficult, but this morning, nothing could bother him. He was feeling good!

Somewhere in the back of his mind, something was trying to tell him not to be too happy. Life could be very tricky. Just when you think you have it made....

Anyway, he wasn't going to think of things like that now. He was young, strong, alive...the air was fresh and clean and crisp, and he decided to try contacting Freye Hunnicutt, a buddy from Nam days. He lived in a small pad in Brooklyn with his lady. Mac hailed a cab, feeling like a big spender, and being in a hurry to get back to his own "lady". Wow! He felt like a man again!

Twenty minutes later, he stepped out of the cab on Second street in Brooklyn. He paid the cabbie, giving a more generous tip than he was usually wont to do, and checked his address book again.

The landlady shut the door none too politely, after having notified him that nobody named Hunnicutt lived in her apartment house, nor had for the five years she had been managing. Mac turned away and stood thinking for a moment or two. Where now?

Fifteen minutes, and a half dozen phone calls later, he was once again in a cab on his way to the Bowery. He had been given the name of a dealer by Tom Washburn, another Nam Vet who had been in his battalion. Tom had been reluctant at first to admit he was still using, but the urgency Mac expressed, and the assurances of secrecy he repeated, finally got through, and Mac was launched on the second, by no means easiest lap, of his delicate mission.

The cab pulled up in front of a small Chinese restaurant, The Golden Dragon, which appeared, though small and inexpensive, to be the epitome of respectability. Mac knew, however, that this was hostile territory—not part of the world, he was used to dealing in. He thanked God for the toughening process of his stint in the service. He knew he would need all the lessons he had learned in Nam to carry him through the next few days. He had been hatching up some tentative plans in the cab.

Getting the opium was not too bad, as long as he kept his head and played it cool. The worst part of the whole thing was that he knew Kim would somehow have to be cured of her addiction so that she could lead a normal life again. That is providing they both came out of this thing in one piece. The thing that did scare him a little was the sure knowledge that Kim would never be free to live any kind of life as long as this Kai Ching and his remaining henchmen were on the loose. But that was the next step—one at a time was more than sufficient.

He asked the driver to wait, and then found his way around to the back of the restaurant. It was already getting dark, although it was still fairly early in the evening. The days were getting shorter, and he, being a sun worshiper, always hated the end of summer and the coming of autumn, a sure sign of the cold, dark, dreary days of winter.

He approached the small, dingy back door, illuminated by a dirty yellow 25-watt bulb which hung precariously from a rusty nail. He knocked in the "three, plus one, plus two" pattern that Tom Washburn had given him, then waited. Nothing. He tried it again, and caught himself holding his breath. He took in a deep breath and tried to loosen some of the tension in his neck and shoulders.

It seemed like ages before the door creaked open and an old, wrinkled Asian face peered out at him through the narrow aperture. He was pleased with the normal sound of his voice as he spoke, for it belied the qualms that were shaking up his intestines.

The man just stood there, silently, so Mac ventured, "I'd like a pipeful—the good stuff. I was told I could get it here."

"Don't know what you talk about," the old man said, starting to close the door.

"Wait!" Mac blurted, remembering the added information Tom had given him.

"The poppies are beautiful this time of year."

The pressure on the door lessened, and the old man stared at him closely for another moment, then he opened the door enough for Mac to push through. The interior was a dimly lit hallway. He could feel the warmth and smell the aromas of oriental food.

Five minutes later he was back in the taxi, the opium stashed carefully in his jacket pocket and a large bag of oriental food sat in his lap—the wonderful smells of the different dishes mingling together to make his empty stomach growl loudly.

He stopped at his door, almost afraid to open it and find that this whole thing was just a dream, a figment of his lonely imagination.

He breathed easier, as a few minutes later he watched Kim satisfy her dependency on the weed. She smiled, lazily as she leaned back in the easy chair, the blanket still wrapped around her. She was beautiful again, now relaxed, drowsy and infinitely desirable.

Mac warmed up the Chinese dinner, and they both ate ravenously. She placed her elbows on the table and gazed at him, wonderingly.

"Why are you doing all this for me, Mac? You've taken great risks right from the first. Why did you follow me into that alley? No one takes chances like that to help strangers."

"I don't know, honey, just a big pushover, I guess I just never could stand by and watch people get hurt. I always get my hackles up when I find some bully picking on someone half his size," he explained.

"That may explain your attack on Hermann but why bring me here to your own apartment? Why risk your neck getting me fixed up?" she persisted.

"I think I told you the reason before I left this morning. But perhaps in the condition you were in, you didn't hear me," he smiled.

"I thought I heard you, but I couldn't credit what I was hearing. People don't fall in love that quickly especially with some strange woman one rescues from an alley after she's shot a man," she said.

"Not even if she shot that man to save your neck? Not even if she's the most beautiful, sensual female you've ever laid eyes on, and not if you've been searching all your life to find such a woman?"

"Not even if she gave herself to you as if she were a whore—without even knowing your name??" she flashed back at him, lowering her head so as not to see the expression in his eyes.

"That's something I never want to hear from you again, young lady," he scolded. "What happened between us was a rare and beautiful thing. It was natural and right—and when I get back tonight, I'm going to do everything in my power to make it happen again and again."

"Get back?!" She got up quickly, the blanket slipping off her, exposing the beauty of her uplifted young breasts to his eager gaze. "But where are you going now?"

He couldn't resist cupping the softness of her breasts in his hands as he kissed her. "I have some business to attend to," he explained. "I want you to stay right here and get some rest. I won't be gone too long, and you'll need all of your energy when I get back," he laughed as he playfully took one of her breasts in his mouth and fondled it with his tongue.

As he kissed her, she moaned with happiness, and grabbed him close to her, pressing the now erected tips of her breasts against his chest. "Hurry back," she whispered, kissing him on the neck. "I promise to be very energetic!"

"Now, how am I going to leave? My dick is loaded, and what will all the little old ladies on the street think when I walk out with my trousers sticking straight out in front?".

They both laughed, and he pulled himself reluctantly from her grasp. He reached down and picked up the blanket from the floor at their feet and placed it lovingly around her shoulders, gazing at her body longingly until the last second.

Closing and locking the door behind him for the second time that day, he paused, his body tied up in knots, his manhood throbbing. Thinking it the better part of valor, he went down the hall to the public men's room, and relieved his swollen member. It was just too damned big to be walking around with it when it was loaded.

His appointment was for 7:30 that night…he had a half-hour to get there.

CHAPTER Six

It seemed like ages he'd been waiting in the small, dingy outer office. A fly—the large, black, noisy variety—had been buzzing around him frantically since his arrival. He wondered how long it could keep up its attack without coming to rest somewhere. He had to stop watching it, but somehow his eyes were glued to its frantic gyrations. Suddenly it came zooming at him in a kamikaze dive. He moved quickly, and the fly hit the wall behind his head with great force. The buzzing stopped. The silence was deafening.

"Mac Neely?"

The voice out of the silence startled him and he jumped. He hadn't realized just how uptight he was.

A skinny, bald-headed man who had poked his head out of a door marked "Investigation," summoned him into an even smaller, and if possible, dingier office.

"Inspector Lindham will see you now," the bald-headed man intoned.

The man sitting behind the old wooden desk was tall, at least from what Mac could see of him, and somewhat attractive—in a macho way. He laid down a small pocket knife with which he had been doddle-carving on the old desk top. The entire surface of the desk was covered with initials, hearts, arrows, and all sorts of geometrical designs. Mac looked up from the handiwork on the desk into the calm blue eyes of agent Dan Lindham. Mac judged him to be in his early thirties and was later on to learn that 10 of those years had been spent as an agent for the Federal Bureau of Investigation.

"Yes, sir," Lindham smiled. "Something I can do for you?"

"I sure hope so," Mac answered. "I really appreciate you seeing me this late, but I just couldn't take a chance on waiting until tomorrow. The safety of a young woman is involved."

"No problem. Mr...McNeely, is it?"

"Yes, but you can call me Mac." He hesitated, then plunged in. "I wasn't really sure whether I should risk bringing the FBI into this, but I'm just an ordinary citizen. I don't feel I have the know-how to handle something as big as this seems to be."

"We're pretty good with protection, Mac. I, personally, have had a lot of experience with kidnap cases, and they are about as tricky as you can get when it comes to protecting the victim."

He indicated the rickety-looking chair by his desk, and Mac seated himself gingerly, his large muscular form posing a real threat to the stability of his perch. Mac looked at Lindham for a moment or 3 two before he started to speak. He was pretty good at sizing people up—bartenders get that way after a while—and he sensed that this young man knew his business. What's more, he liked the calm, efficient aura and the modest good looks of agent Dan Lindham. He decided to trust him.

Mac told Lindham the whole story, trying not to leave out the smallest detail, (except, of course, for what had transpired in his king-size bed) starting with the moment he had seen the girl rush into the alleyway with the large man on her heels.

Lindham listened attentively, interposing a pertinent question from time to time, and taking notes, until Mac got to the part about Kai Ching. Mac could see Lindham's immediate change of attitude, and the avid interest he now expressed.

Mac concluded, "I know she could be a most valuable witness. She knows this Kai Ching's methods, and a lot of his contacts."

Lindham was quiet for a long moment, then "What makes you think she will be willing to be a witness against this man—her lover?"

"Ex-lover...You don't have to worry about that. She feels no loyalty toward him. She knows her life is in danger, but I know she has guts enough to take a stand against him. The only thing ·I would have to be sure of is that she's protected at all times. Also...I want to know where she stands—legally—in this mess."

"From what you've been telling me, Mac," Lindham replied, "she was just a child when Ching got a hold of her. Other than acting as a messenger, she hasn't done anything too serious. I don't think, if she turned state's evidence, she'd have to serve any time, however... we must tread softly. You could be in a lot of trouble yourself with the locals...accessory after the fact...after all, she is a fugitive mixed up in a street murder. We can protect you to a degree, but the local law enforcement people don't look too kindly on our interference in their jurisdiction. You're treading on pretty thin ice."

"Only too true," Mac admitted. "But she has to be protected at all cost. These men are dangerous, the type who'd stop at nothing."

Lindham looked searchingly at Mac. "It sounds like you have become emotionally involved with this girl. Are you in love with her?"

"I've asked myself the same question. I know the feelings I have for her are strong enough that I don't want to take a chance on losing her," Mac admitted.

"Well, if she is instrumental in catching Ching and his cohorts, it will weigh heavily in her favor. In the meantime, we'll do all we can to see she is kept out of Ching's clutches."

"Then what's our next move? I'm ready to do all I can to assist your department."

"Good," Lindham smiled. "Then, I think our next move is to tell your whole story again to my boss, Inspector Greer. It just so happens that this is his baby. He has been trying to get something on Kai Ching for a long time now. I think I can assure you; he will be more than eager to get this information. There's more going on with Ching than just the international drug trafficking...something very heavy... heavy enough to make the drug pushing seem like teeter-totter time."

The talk with Greer had gone well, and although Mac was tiring and his brain getting fuzzier by the minute, he picked up a lot of information on Kai and his activities. He left feeling much more confident that it would not be long before Kim would be safe from danger. Then it would only be a matter of getting her clear of the weed and...well, who knew what the future might hold.

Mac wondered again at the emotions he was experiencing. "So," he thought elatedly, "this is what living is all about." This elation over a woman and her lovely, gracefully sensuous body...this tingle of anticipation...the total awareness and, not the least of it all, the danger lurking in the background. Mac wondered how he could ever stand again behind his bar—ever again fade into the bar fixtures. He was beginning to realize that there was a real man lurking inside this hull of his, after all a living, breathing, feeling man—and the knowledge of it was good.

CHAPTER

Seven

It was after midnight when he again turned the key in the lock and let himself into his apartment. As he stepped inside the apartment door, the delicious smell of food cooking assailed his nostrils, and he realized that he hadn't eaten since early that evening, and Chinese food is notorious for not staying with you. He was ravenously hungry.

Kim was setting the few plastic dishes he had on the table when he stepped into the kitchenette. She had showered and slipped into one of his T-shirts, which didn't quite come down to cover her rounded, firm bottom, and which was happily thin enough to show the contours of the lovely breasts, with the darker pointed nipples pushing eagerly at the fabric as if wanting to escape their gentle bondage.

She looked up and saw him standing in the doorway, the desire obvious in his eyes. She ran into his arms and pressed her body tightly against his, causing an instant reaction from his awakened manhood. She smelled of Irish Spring and talcum powder, and her hair was soft and gleaming and just slightly damp from its recent shampoo. If he needed any more to turn him on, her freshness and shiny face would do it.

They kissed long and thoroughly, the flames of desire growing stronger with every moment that they stood pressed together in the doorway.

Finally, she broke slowly away, stating breathlessly, "We have to stop for now, or we'll both starve to death. We must get something in our stomachs, and then…." Her smile was a promise of what was to come, and he was going to hold her to it. Hold her to "it", too.

"There wasn't much around here to work with. You must eat out most of the time, huh? I hope you like what I've fixed…and then, I didn't know for sure when you'd be getting home."

"Everything you do is nothing short of phenomenal," he laughed, as they started to the table arm in arm. They both forgot everything else as they eagerly dug into the canned roast beef hash, fried potatoes, and sipped steaming hot coffee. It was not until every bite was cleared from their plates, that they again became aware of each other physically.

The dishes lay unwashed in the sink as he carried her into the bedroom and sank with her onto the bed. The "dessert" she had promised him was well worth waiting for. Both of them refreshed, and possessing renewed strength and vigor, they went about enjoying each other's bodies with great energy and delight.

"This is my kind of dessert," Mac assured her, his tongue busy with her loveliness. "Mmmmm," she moaned in pleasure, "and where is mine?"

He gladly supplied her with his huge, hot manhood…thrilling to the feel of her soft lips and eager tongue. He stretched to reach the lamp by the bed and turned it on so he could feast his eyes on the beauty of her young, passionate body. He turned around so that he could explore her intimate softness as she continued administering to his manhood. He was thrilled as she responded to his tongue, and her spasms of joy made his whole groin area tingle and his member swelled even larger with her gentle lovemaking. When he could handle the pleasure no longer without expelling his seed, he pulled gently away and started exploring every inch of her body, kissing her thighs, her tummy, finding great joy in fondling her tautly erected breasts. She came with ecstatic squeals as he fondled and caressed her body from breasts to buttocks and back again to the sweetness of her mouth, his fingers lingering to do their work in the softness between her thighs.

Her tongue moved over the firm hardness of his nipples, then she ran her hands and mouth over his abdomen and started to shower his manhood with butterfly caresses. The joy of it was almost beyond bearing.

Before he realized what was happening, she had rolled on top of him, slowly lowering herself down on his length of manhood, slowly moving up and down in an even, pulsing rhythm. He watched her face as she made love to him...for as long as he could maintain his senses—then they both started on that fantastic journey to ecstasy.

As they slowly returned to the land of the living (he personally felt more alive in the center of the vortex) they gazed lazily into each other's eyes, in their mutual happiness and satisfaction.

The rest of the night was spent in much the same manner. They would sleep a little, and wake up to renewed desires, which they did not hesitate to satisfy—one way or another—until they were off again down their favorite road to climax-land.

They visited the place so many times that Mac, who was used to one trip a night, at best, with other women, was totally exhausted by the wee hours of the morning.

As he sank finally into a deep, exhausted, druglike sleep, he noticed Kim sitting up and looking at him intently.

"She must be tired," he mused to himself as he sank into a much-needed oblivion. When he thought about it later, he had to admit that she hadn't looked tired at all. She was apparently insatiable, and he really didn't mind the fact too much. Yes, she was a most unusual woman.

Something smelled good, his sleepy mind acknowledged, as he awoke to find she was not beside him. He panicked for a moment, but relaxed as he heard her humming as she came into the room bearing a tray laden with eggs, bacon, toast, and a steaming cup of hot coffee.

"Morning, sleepyhead," she chirped happily. "Or should I say 'good afternoon'?"

His head clearing, he looked hurriedly at his watch. It was almost noon. "My God, I have to be out of here in half an hour." He started eating quickly, enjoying every bite.

"Where did the food come from?" he asked, suddenly remembering his empty larder.

"Oh, I sneaked out to the corner market this morning and replenished our stores. I picked your pocket...hope you don't mind," she laughed.

Alarmed, he scolded her. "You went out alone!? Do you know how dangerous that was? Don't ever do that again, do you hear me!"

Looking only slightly repentant, she came back at him, "Okay, worry-wart, but I don't see how they could trace me here. They don't even know who you are."

"Just the same, we're not taking any chances. Until we get this thing cleared up, I want you locked in this apartment.

"I know it won't be easy for you, but we just can't take any chances. My dick would go into a coma if I lost you now," he laughed, not wanting to alarm her too much.

"You keep talking like that, and I'll give you your dessert right in the middle of breakfast," she giggled, reaching for his manhood, which was already hard in anticipation.

"Not now, honey. I've got this appointment, and it may mean the difference between a future for us, or not."

She looked at him intently, her eyes filling with anxiety again. "Mac, what are you up to? Where were you last night? It had to do with me, didn't it? You've got to tell me. I'm the one who got you into all this."

He told her about his trip to the FBI, of Lindham and Greer, and explained to her that he would be working closely with them to put Kai Ching away where he belonged.

Her reaction startled him. She was literally terrified! Her glowing face once again was drawn and pale.

"No, no, Mac! You can't get any more involved! They'll kill you, too." Tears streamed down her face. "Oh, what have I done? What have I gotten you into?" she wailed.

"We're both in this together, baby. Fate brought us together, and from now on, everything that we do will be together. Do you understand what I'm saying?"

"Oh, Mac!" She threw herself into his arms. "Mac, I do love you so. I love you so much it hurts. Dear God, if something were to happen to you now"

"Don't worry, honey. I can take care of myself—and you too for that matter." He slipped quickly into his clothes. "I should be back in an hour or so. Have to meet with Lindham. Keep the door locked, and don't for any reason go out of this apartment again! Got that!?" She grinned her agreement.

"Now, where the heck did I put that gun?"

"Mac," she cried. "Why do you need a gun?"

"It's okay. Lindham wants it...evidence, I guess."

He located it in the front room where he had dropped it as he had carried Kim's unconscious body to the couch. It had slipped down between the cushions. He used his handkerchief to pick it up, as Lindham had instructed, and stuck it, wrapped in the handkerchief, into his jacket pocket.

Thus prepared, he gave her a very quick kiss, not wanting to have to make a stop at the men's room down the hall, and quickly locked her securely in the apartment. He took the stairs two at a time, the gun feeling heavy and unfamiliar next to his heart.

CHAPTER

Eight

The afternoon was spent in making plans with Greer and Lindham. When Mac departed the FBI office, he was fairly satisfied that the plans were good ones, and that it would not be long before Kai and his men were behind bars.

As he rounded the corner toward the cab stand, he stiffened as he felt a hard, sharp object pressed against his ribs. "Don't look around," a high-pitched Asian voice hissed into his ear. "Just keep walking. That maroon car over there. Get in and keep your mouth shut."

Not valuing the merits of bravado, Mac quickly obeyed. He slid into the empty backseat of the maroon Chevy, noting the satisfied smile on the face of the driver. The man with the knife slipped quietly in beside Mac, settling himself so that the knife rested gently against Mac's rib cage. As the door of the car slammed shut, the driver, a surly-looking thug who was no longer smiling, took off in a flurry of screeching tires and roaring motor.

"If this wasn't so frighteningly real," thought Mac, "it would really be too cliché. Do they actually still take people for rides?"

He ventured the question aloud to his knife-wielding companion and was answered by stony silence. He knew instinctively, and from Kim's description that this must be Kai's second-in-charge henchman…what was the name again?… "Oh yes, Kato. An extremely ugly bastard," Mac thought, with a face out of some long-forgotten nightmare.

Kato was of small build, wiry and slightly misshapen, as many of the older generation Asian men tended to be. His face was a mask of taut yellowing skin stretched tightly over a flat, high cheekboned facial structure. He wore a wispy mustache and a pointed, equally wispy beard. But the feature that stood out most was a long, evil-looking scar that ran from forehead to chin across the left side of his face. It was red and angry looking, even though, on close inspection, one could see it was not a new addition. The eyes that now turned to glare at him contained the epitome of the spirit of evil.

"Where are you taking me? Or is that too much to ask?" Mac queried. All he got for an answer was a look so bleak that he was forced to turn his face away. The scenery, though familiar, was a pleasant alternative. They drove on through the crowded Manhattan streets for what seemed to Mac an endless time; then finally headed south and joined the heavy traffic on the Hudson River Parkway. The scenery changed now, and as it spun by was so varied and interesting that Mac was able to lose himself in it for a time. At first, he tried to memorize their movements, but finally realized that the driver was deliberately backtracking and circling to confuse him, so gave up the effort. The ride was beginning to seem interminable.

Mac ventured another question to Kato, but after receiving the same unsatisfactory results, he gave up and leaned back against the seat to wait, the knife still poking painfully into his ribs when he moved too quickly to suit Kato.

After approximately another half hour's ride, the driver pulled the maroon Chevy into a circular driveway and stopped before the large, ornate doors of a huge old Victorian-style mansion. Kato motioned him out with the knife that he still held efficiently in his left hand.

Recognizing the futility of resistance, Mac got out and followed Kato, who led the way up the broad staircase and rang the bell cord which hung in antique splendor to the right of the huge carved oak doors. He could feel the eyes of the driver on his back, and it made his flesh crawl to know that nothing would please the man more than to have orders to shoot Mac in the back if he made the slightest move to escape.

The doors swung open slowly, and as if in answer to his hesitation, Mac felt the point of Kato's "pet" again press impatiently against his side, urging him on.

The inside of the mansion was even more impressive than the façade. Mac didn't claim to know much about art, but even he recognized that this old house would be an antique dealer's dream. A few obviously very valuable large pieces of furniture were placed strategically around the entryway, which was graced with a broad staircase that branched out right and left to the second floor. Again, Mac got the feeling of being in an old "B" mystery movie.

Mac was led, or to be more accurate, shoved, into the library, which was the second door on the right of the marbled entryway.

It was just as you would picture a library in this type of relic mansion—its walls filled with shelves of books of every size, color, and description, many he suspected were first editions. Directly in line with the entrance, in front of a pair of large French doors, stood the desk. It was an immense semi-circular modern affair of shining mahogany, which somehow miraculously managed to blend in with the antiquity of the room.

Mac's gaze finally settled on the man who was seated behind the desk. His interest was immediately caught and held, not only by the physical appearance of the man, but by the sheer animal magnetism he exuded. He looked about 35, and was the most unusual mixture of races Mac had ever seen. His face was extremely handsome, and quite Asian, the high cheekbones and fine structure were excelled only by the fine straight Arian nose that was, though out of tune with the Asian look, oddly intriguing. The eyes were gray, and they had a hardness which one would describe as "steely". He wore a small mustache, which was, along with his hair, the most surprising feature of all because they were both quite blond, almost platinum. As Kai stood up, Mac could see that he was a tall man, at least six foot one, and very well built.

Kai smiled, and if Mac hadn't known better, he would have thought that he was an old and close friend who hadn't seen him in years. So charming and warm were both the smile and the handshake which was forced upon him, that he had to remember the things Kim had told him about this man to keep from being put at a disadvantage.

"Mr. Neely, isn't it?" Kai smiled. "We've been waiting for you."

Mac decided it was foolish to try and bluff his way out of this, so he answered, returning charm for charm, "Right. And, you are, of course, Mr. Kai Ching."

"I hope we aren't keeping you from anything important." The charming voice took on a snake-like smoothness as Kai resumed his seat. "Please be seated. I'm afraid we are going to have to detain you for a while. Would you care for a cup of coffee…tea?"

Mac shook his head as he lowered his bulk into the upholstered high back chair in front of the desk. No longer able to restrain his curiosity, Mac asked, "How did you find me?"

"Had you been a little more 'streetwise'," the smooth voice purred, "you would have known that you couldn't have acquired opium anywhere in this country without me knowing about it."

"Did you think we wouldn't be waiting for Kim to send someone to get the stuff for her?"

"I was assured that my transaction would be kept secret. I guess I was a little too naive," Mac admitted. "But that doesn't explain how you found me, or how you knew of my connection with Kim." Mac found himself holding his breath for the answer, knowing that if they had found his address, Kim would be in immediate danger.

As if Kai had read his thoughts, he smiled. "Yes, Mr. Neely, we know where you live. Kim was spotted this morning and followed to your apartment. We've had a man watching your place all day." Kai looked at Mac out of the corner of his slanted grey eyes as he lit a cigarette. "He even followed you to the FBI. That was a very foolish move, Mr. Neely. It only convinced us that we couldn't afford to let you run around free any longer."

Mac drew in a long breath. "And, Kim?"

"You'll be relieved to hear that she is safely here with us." Kai smiled suavely.

"Safe!?" Mac swallowed. The whole scene had a quality of unreality about it. Mac heard his own voice as if at a distance. "Okay, what in the hell are you up to? What do you intend to do with us?"

"Oh, you are both quite safe...for the time being. Neither of you will be hurt until we find out how much you have involved us with the FBI." Kai eyed Mac frankly, taking in his rugged good looks and giving grudging admiration to Mac's reactions to this whole situation. "I suppose you would like to see her," Kai ventured.

"You're damned right I would...and she'd better not be hurt in any way," Mac growled, not being able to hide the anger and jealousy that welled up inside him at the thought of this man's past association with Kim. He grudgingly admitted to himself that he could see why an innocent young girl might be attracted to this extremely handsome snake-in-man's clothing.

Kai pressed a buzzer on the hand-carved, gleaming desk, and then reached for an ornate silver cigarette box. After lighting a new cigarette from the stub held between his lips, he proffered the box to Mac.

"No thanks. I can think of quicker ways to commit suicide," Mac came back.

"You don't mind if I indulge, do you?" Kai smiled.

"It's your funeral, or is that wishful thinking?" Mac quipped, matching Kai's smile.

Kai inhaled deeply, then chuckled. He rose as the door behind Mac opened. Mac rose automatically, turning to see Kim being shoved through the door by a grim Kato.

"Mac!" Kim cried, as she broke away from Kato and ran to throw herself into Mac's arms. Mac forgot everything for a moment in his relief and joy to be holding his precious jewel in his arms again. He kissed her wildly and she returned his kisses with the force of passion he had found in no other woman.

"A very pretty picture, don't you agree, Kato?" The snake-like voice interrupted the two lovers. Kato just looked from the couple to his boss, and the evil there in his eyes spoke for itself. "You may go, Kato. I don't think I'll have any trouble from these two." Kato reluctantly complied, leaving the three people who were caught in the age-old triangle alone in the huge old library. Mac stared with hostility at Kai, Kim watching his face as he did so. Kai just stood there behind the desk, smiling at them in a knowing manner that brought the bile to Mac's throat. No one spoke. The suspense grew as the ornate, carved clock on the mantle ticked away the minutes.

"You needn't look so worried, old man," Kai soothed. "I'm not jealous. My interest in Kim died long ago. I get bored easily with my toys." Kim stiffened in Mac's arms and he gave her a reassuring squeeze.

"Then why are you holding us?" Mac growled.

"Surely you're not as naive as all that," Kai drawled. "Kim is in a position to do us a great deal of harm. I shudder to think of what could have happened to me if my operations had not been able to locate you two before Kim could testify against me."

"And you can't be as naive as to think you can get away with this. The FBI has been on to you for a long time. If we disappear, they'll know who's responsible," Mac parried.

"Unfortunately, that won't be much help to you two, now will it?" Kai smiled, and for the first time since Mac had arrived, the charm couldn't hide the evil behind that smile. "But now, I would imagine you two would like to be alone for a bit."

Mac could see that Kai was holding in some secret enjoyment.

It was almost as if he, Mac, was being laughed at. Well, he had to admit, he hadn't been too clever about this whole affair. He wished he felt more like laughing at himself, but looking down at Kim, so young and helpless in his arms, he had never felt less like laughing.

Kai, remaining cool, continued. "We have a suite of rooms prepared for you. You can have your meals sent up to you, or, if you prefer, you can join me in the dining room. I do get rather lonesome at times," he smiled warmly, the picture of the charming host.

Mac tightened his arm around Kim and replied, "We prefer our own company, thank you. We don't want to take unfair advantage of your warm and friendly hospitality." He smiled his gratitude with a smile as deadly mocking as the one they had received from Kai.

"Very well, then. It's your choice. Though I must confess I was rather looking forward to hearing some of the stories you've picked up behind the bar. It must be fascinating work, fascinating!" Kai reached for the buzzer.

Kato must have been waiting right outside the door, for he appeared instantly and deadpan as ever he led Mac and Kim up the broad staircase on the right, down a curving hallway, and opened a heavy door at the end to expose a large living room, exquisitely and expensively furnished in what Mac guessed was about the Louis XIV style.

Kato silently closed the door behind them, and Mac could hear the bolt as it settled into place. Superfluously, he reached back and tried the door, and was not surprised to find it locked. He shrugged and then took Kim into his arms again, giving her a kiss and a reassuring hug. He then decided to inspect their fancy prison, hardly hopeful of finding a chink in Kai's protective accommodations.

The windows, as he had expected, were barred. There was a comfortably large bedroom through the door on his right, a walk-in closet on his left, and a large bathroom that opened to both rooms.

Kim's curiosity had led her to the closet, and she let out a gasp of surprise when she opened it to find a large array of women's clothes. "Mac," she squealed. "They're mine. They're my clothes that I left behind. He doesn't miss a trick, does he?"

"He doesn't seem to have been too worried about your getting away." As he spoke, Mac opened the door to a small closet near the bathroom. "A considerate host, indeed." He sighed as he examined a whole row of men's suits, all his size, and all with expensive name labels.

"Kai believes in fattening the lambs before the slaughter, I guess," Kim acknowledged. "He was never negligent in his solicitude for my 'physical' needs," she added, not being able to keep the bitter sarcasm from creeping into her voice.

She stood there in front of the closet filled with expensive clothes—in the magnificently decorated suite, and looked at Mac helplessly. "Oh, Mac!" she cried, breaking down for the first time, tears flowing from her beautiful almond shaped eyes. "Why couldn't I have met you first? Now it's over before it's even begun."

Mac moved quickly to her and held her close to him, rocking her gently from side to side, murmuring reassurances. "Hey, now wait, honey. Don't be giving up so easily. The FBI is on to this guy. They're bound to do something to help us."

He nestled his cheek against her soft, silky black hair, breathing in the perfume of it.

"Oh, Mac," she cried, "What can they do? In the first place, they don't even know Kai has us, and even if they did, they don't know where. I've never even seen this place before. I haven't the least notion where we are." The tears welled up again. "Oh, Mac. I'm so frightened. And... I do love you so."

His heart thumped madly against his ribs. To hear this beautiful, desirable woman speak of loving him made him feel ten feet tall. In spite of the place, the danger they were in, or maybe because of it, he felt his eager manhood growing and pressing up against her lovely young body.

Kim felt it too, and instantly her tears stopped, and she pressed herself eagerly against him, arching to feel every inch of his hardened shaft against her.

He took her right there on the thick carpeting of the bedroom, not taking time to lift her onto the large-canopied bed.

There was a kind of desperation in their love-making this time that heightened every sensation. They made love as if there would be no tomorrow, and who knew if there would be?

Her tongue was frenetic in its explorations, and the sensations it provoked in him were painfully good. Oh, yes, such lovely pain. He never wanted her to stop, and he returned her gift with his own tongue, as he explored the secret sweetness between her thighs. He took great joy in making her come again and again. Then he mounted her and found his own fulfillment. They relaxed then, and after a few moments, he began to kiss her, very gently and sweetly, pouring into her all his gratitude for the joy she gave him. Soon they were at the point of fulfilment again. He was always amazed that with her, as with no other woman, he got one erection after another, never seeming to get enough of her sweetness.

When their excitement and joy had finally exhausted them, he lifted her onto the bed and lay down beside her. They were quickly in a deep and healing sleep—a mercifully forgetful sleep, bodies closely entwined, two heads close together, two textures of black hair intermingled on the pillow—two young people, very much in love and very much in trouble.

CHAPTER Nine

It must have been two hours later when Mac was awakened by a sharp knock on the living room door. He grabbed his trousers, and hopping around, got into them on the way to the door.

As he was zipping his fly, a sour faced woman holding a large tray, unlocked the door just as he reached it. The aroma of roast beef made him realize how ravenously hungry he was. An armed guard stood behind the woman, who Mac assumed was some kind of housekeeper, waiting watchfully as she placed the tray on the coffee table in front of a long couch.

Mac thanked the woman, who rewarded him with a dirty look, and as she departed, he heard the bolt once more dropped into place. Mac carried the tray into the bedroom, and held it near to Kim's sleeping face. It didn't take long for the aroma to rouse her, and she clapped her hands joyfully in a childlike exuberance, as they dug into the tender roast beef, baked potatoes, and mixed vegetables. There was steaming hot coffee, and a still-warm raspberry turnover for dessert. Though they praised their host's fare, they couldn't resist a good chuckle when Mac said he preferred the kind of dessert she has served him at his apartment. They spent the rest of the night alternatively making love and sleeping, giving in to whatever urge was the strongest at the moment.

Mac woke before her in the morning light, and lay there with his arm around her, trying to figure out how they were going to get out of this mess. The more he conjectured, the more discouraged he became. He slipped his arm gently out from under Kim's head, trying not to awaken her, and quickly got out of bed and went to the window.

He stood for a long time at the window, feeling the chill of the morning air creeping into his bones. The situation looked even bleaker in the light of day. He could now see that the mansion was surrounded by high, brambled walls, and that there were armed guards at close intervals around these walls. Even if they could get out of the house, how in the hell were they to get past the guards and over those walls? Mac had a strong suspicion that there might also be guard dogs to contend with, knowing the detailed efficiency of his host.

Mac looked back at the warm, innocent girl sleeping so trustingly on the big bed. His heart sank. What could he do to help her? How could he justify the faith she had in him to save them both from Kai Ching? He was just a Manhattan bartender, not versed in the ways of the underworld let alone the international underworld.

He wished his brain would function like the heroes in the dime novels, and he could easily outsmart the villain and carry off the heroin to live happily ever after. But frankly, he was scared. Scared spitless, and feeling very, very helpless and un-macho at the moment. He knew that in action, he would be brave. He had proved that to himself in Nam. But it was this inaction—this not knowing what to do next—that left him feeling so deeply frustrated... and angry with himself.

His body wanted to forget it all. Pretend they were safe in his apartment. He ached to wake Kim and continue their lovemaking, but he knew that wouldn't get them out of the "Dilemma."

He dressed quickly and went into the living room where he silently paced the floor. "Why aren't they making their move? What are they waiting for?" he worried.

As he turned to retrace his steps, he spotted a fancy French telephone on a stand partially hidden behind a large rubber tree plant.

He wondered how he had missed seeing it the night before. Scarcely hoping, he lifted the receiver and dialed for the operator.

"Yes?" Came a woman's cold voice on the other end of the line.

Mac's heart jumped. "Is this the operator?" he asked, holding his breath.

"This is the housekeeper. Are you ready for your breakfast?" was the disappointing, but not totally unexpected reply.

Mac decided to jump in headfirst—taking refuge in action. "No, not yet, thank you. I'd like to speak to Kai Ching—right away—alone!" he demanded.

"I'll give him your message sir."

"Oh, and you might bring some breakfast up to the young lady."

"Right away, sir," the cold voice replied.

Then Mac heard the phone click as she hung up. He went back to his pacing, trying to think up some reason for the upcoming meeting with Kai. He needed some kind of a plan to stall any action Kai might have in mind until help could reach them. "But, what??"

His bare feet sank into the plush flowered carpeting as he moved, his brows were furrowed by the depth of his thoughts. In spite of himself, he jumped when the telephone jangled. He grabbed it quickly so that it would not awaken Kim. He didn't want her trying to stop him, or try to go with him. He wanted this interview to be private. The housekeeper told him that he was to meet Kai in the garden in five minutes.

The guard would be informed to let him out and provide an escort. As he pulled on his socks and shoes, he wondered what he was going to say to this man who seemed to hold all the cards.

Five minutes later, he had the chance to find out, as he once more stood face to face with his new-found, and most deadly enemy.

"Let's walk in the garden, shall we?" smiled Kai. "It's much too beautiful a morning to stay cooped up in this old relic of a house."

If Mac hadn't known what this man did for a living, he would have sworn he was an innocent country gentleman out for his daily constitutional. The charm of the man was uncanny, and it was rare indeed that the mask slipped, and the serpent bared its fangs.

Fortunately, Kai seemed to be in no hurry to get to the point, and the few minutes of respite was a blessing to Mac. They walked slowly, the sun, warming now, beat down on their backs. The garden was incredibly beautiful. Mac could see they had been landscaped by an expert. He was no horticulturist, so he couldn't put names on the flowers that grew in abundance around him. There was an enormous variety of flowers and plants that were entirely new to him, but he did recognize and appreciate the many types and colors of roses that lined the path. Some were almost the size of dinner plates, and the air was filled with their perfume. Bees buzzed gently in the warmth of the sun, giving one a false sense of peace and security.

The soft deep voice interrupted his thoughts. "Do you like flowers, Mr. Neely?"

"Yeah, sure. They're okay."

"I tend these myself, personally. It's sort of a hobby with me. I won't let anyone else touch the roses."

Again, that feeling of unreality.

"These are my own hybrid discovery. I crossed an American Beauty Rose with a Pink Camellia. No one has ever been able to get that particular combination to take before. But I did it." One could not miss the note of pride in Kai's voice as he gently fondled a large varicolored blossom that they had stopped before.

"Very nice." Mac mumbled, tired now of this small talk.

Sensing Mac's impatience, Kai smiled. "I hope you spent a pleasant night. We tried to make you as comfortable as possible."

"Everything was fine," Mac growled.

"She is excellent in bed, isn't she? But then, she should be. I trained her personally."

Mac felt the blood rush up to his face, and it was all he could do to keep from socking this smiling idol in that handsome face of his.

Kai noted his expression. "I'm sure you realize that there are armed men all around us. One move on your part, and I will be so unhappy as to have them shoot you on the spot. You do understand my predicament, don't you?" he insinuated. "Don't, please, force my hand at this point. I would sadly regret losing your company so soon. I am so much enjoying your little love affair with Kim."

Mac took in a deep gulp of fresh morning air and clasped and unclasped his fists, but made no other move—fighting for every ounce of control he displayed.

Kai's smile relaxed. "Now, that's better. What is it you wanted to talk to me about, my friend?"

"Don't call me 'friend'," Mac rasped wishing he could control his emotions as well as the suave degenerate beside him.

"Oh, I'm sorry. 'Mr. Neely,' is that better?... Well, come now, you must realize that my time is valuable."

Mac wrestled with the tread of an idea he had hatched while being led to the garden by the guard.

"You know you can't do anything to harm us," he ventured boldly.

"And why ever not, pray tell?" Kai smiled.

"We're not quite as stupid as you give us credit for. You must realize that we knew there was a possibility you would find us before we got to you. We naturally have insurance," Mac bluffed.

"And what form does this 'insurance' take?" Kai queried.

"For one thing, we have the gun. That is, the FBI has it. I turned it over to them yesterday."

Kai laughed, "Oh, and what is that supposed to insure."

"They're tracing the registration now," Mac parried.

"And what do you suppose they'll find? If it was registered, which it isn't, it would be registered to a Mr. Harry Gunther, recently deceased, and blessedly beyond the long arms of the law."

Mac knew it had been a flimsy try. His brain worked fast, struggling to come up with something more convincing. "That's not too important, anyway. Just thought I'd throw it in for openers. The real insurance is the dossier."

"Dossier?"

"Yes. But, don't worry, it's in a safe place," Mac threw in.

"No doubt. But safe from what? What is this 'dossier' that you are so enthralled with?" Kai parried, seemingly totally indifferent.

"Only a complete account of all your activities in the past five years. Enough to put your organization out of business, and you behind bars for the rest of your life," Mac bluffed wildly.

Kai laughed. "Sorry if I'm not taking this too seriously, but I really doubt that you took enough time from your romancing to put together such a dossier. And, if you had, why would you not have taken it to the FBI with the gun?" Kai replied assuredly.

Mac improvised quickly. "Then it wouldn't have been any use to us. We had to have some bargaining power with the FBI to get Kim off the hook, plus we needed the insurance in case something like this should happen."

"Why, my dear fellow. 'Something like this?' Whatever do you mean? You two are simply guests in my home for a few days. You are, I believe, finding everything to your satisfaction, aren't you? The suite…the food?" Kai mocked. "We're making every effort to accommodate you."

"You bastard!" Mac hissed through his teeth. "You know what I mean. If either of us is killed, the dossier will automatically be mailed to the FBI. They'll have all the proof they need."

"My dear fellow. I'm afraid all they would have is a letter from a dead woman who couldn't corroborate it. No proof whatsoever."

Mac's brain spun like a computer bank. "I'm sorry to disappoint you, Mr. Ching, but there is plenty of proof in that envelope. Do you think Kim ran away empty-handed?"

Mac was pleased to note a flicker of doubt flash in Kai's Asian eyes, then as quickly disappear.

"Among other things," he continued, "you will remember that you were kind enough to provide Kim with an excellent college education. Part of that education was a course in photography, and she learned extremely well. Yes, she has taken some really excellent photographs of some very incriminating documents."

"I must compliment you, Mr. Neely. You are really an excellent bluffer. Comes from your years as a bartender, I would suspect."

"You wish that I was bluffing," Mac smiled, enjoying his moment of being in control of the situation, even if it was built on his imagination.

"It is totally impossible for there to be any such photographs," Kai countered gruffly. "Such documents as you speak of, if such documents existed, would be kept in my safe, which I can assure you is burglar-proof. She would have no way of getting to them."

"It's an interesting thing about quiet, unassuming women. They can be around at the most unexpected moments, and you might not even notice them. Kim, if you will think back, was near you many times when you opened that safe. She has very good eyes and an even better memory."

Mac's shot in the dark hit its mark. Kai's face dropped its mask of geniality for a moment. He turned away from Mac and broke one of the larger rose blossoms, bringing the flower up to his face where he inhaled deeply of its scent. When he faced Mac again, the ingratiating smile was back.

"At any rate," he spoke softly, "I had no immediate plans for eliminating the two of you. I'm enjoying your visit too much. I really find you very amusing." Quite amazingly, Kai reverted to the country gentleman again as he resumed his guided tour of the gardens, naming the different varieties and pointing out several species of very rare cacti. This was undoubtedly a baffling man. Mac had no idea if his bluff was going to be successful or not.

Finally, Kai stopped and looked at his watch. "Please forgive me for being rude, old fellow, but I really must get cracking. Was there anything else I could do for you?"

"One little thing, yes. It seems you found it necessary to get Kim hooked. When she wakes up, she'll need some of the damned 'Poppy'."

"Not to worry, old man. She took a generous supply with her breakfast. I think you'll find her in fine fettle when you get back." He led Mac to the back door where a guard was awaiting him. "You should be very grateful to me, actually. The stuff tends to make our little lady extremely loving. At least," he grinned at Mac knowingly, "I always found it so."

Mac turned his back on him and joined the guard. He didn't dare stay with this garden snake or he'd surely bash his considerably large fist into his handsome face. He followed the guard without a backward glance. It would be good to get back to the suite, prison or not.

CHAPTER

Ten

The guard bolted the door behind Mac and he was once again a helpless victim, feeling more frustrated and angrier than ever. He was surprised that Kim had not met him at the door, and noticing her untouched breakfast tray on the coffee table, he called to her. There was no answer. Mac felt fear rising up into his throat, gagging him. He rushed into the bedroom and found Kim on the floor beside the bed, shaking and moaning in her need for the poppy which had her at its mercy.

He quickly picked her up and held her close to his body. She was so cold. He never knew anyone could be that cold and still be alive. He sat on the edge of the bed and pulled a blanket up around her, cursing Kai under his breath. He held her body close and crooned consoling words into her ear as she cried out in pain.

"I thought Kai said he'd taken care of you, damn his filthy soul—if he has one!" Mac carried her into the living room and sitting on the couch with her, grabbed the phone.

"Yes. Yes, you sure can help. Get that bastard on this phone right now! Gone?! Where...when will he be back?... Well, Ms. Henri needs something he promised she would have, and it can't wait!... What?... on the breakfast tray?... No, no, she didn't eat breakfast. I guess she didn't see it. Okay, thanks. I'll take care of it." Mac hung up the phone and reached over to take the dome off the breakfast tray. Just as the housekeeper had said, the dope was there in a neat little package.

Mac had his hands full for the next few minutes as Kim thrashed and tossed—crying out for his help, hardly aware that he was satisfying her need.

He soothed her as best he could until finally the drug took effect and she calmed down, nestling against his chest, her dark head on his shoulder, sleeping peacefully. He held her like that until she finally awoke two hours later.

She opened her beautiful eyes slowly. She looked so innocent and childlike, Mac thought. How could anyone be unkind to such a lovely young person? Anger burned in him again, and he let out an expletive.

Kim, fully awake now, looked at him in surprise. "Oh, Mac, honey, you're here. I was so worried about you. Is something wrong? You're angry."

"Not with you, honeybun. Just in general," Mac assured her.

"But where did you go? I was so worried." She sat up and faced him. "That bitch wouldn't tell me a thing when she brought my breakfast. I thought they...I thought you were..." Her lips trembled and her eyes grew wide.

Mac melted. This woman was more than he could ever have hoped for. He pulled her close and held her, planting small tender kisses in her hair. "I'm fine, honey. Really great now that you're feeling better," he murmured.

"But where were you?" Kim urged.

Mac outlined his meeting with Kai, and she listened with great interest. When he told her about faking the stolen document bit, she gasped, and her hand flew to her throat.

"Honey! What is it? What's the matter? Are you in pain?" Mac grabbed her two cold hands and held them between his large warm ones.

"But...but how could you have known about the documents?" she cried. "I purposely didn't tell you so as not to endanger you more," she admitted.

"You don't mean to tell me you do have proof? That's just too far out."

"I did tell you that I could incriminate him. You don't think I would trust anyone to take my word alone?" She blurted. "Christ! But...why didn't you tell me?"

"That was silly. I was already in it up to my ears. Hell, I could have taken them to the FBI!"

"I planned on taking them myself. You were already, as you say, involved, but I was sure I could handle it and keep Kai from learning about you. Don't you see, Mac. I realized how much you meant to me, even in such a short time. I couldn't take a chance on getting you killed," she sighed, a tear escaping the corner of her eye.

"Honey, from the first minute I saw you, it was all or nothing. Whatever trouble you're in is my trouble too." His brow furrowed. "But, if you have documents, or photographs, where are they?"

"I have several very important documents on microfilm. The trouble is, the microfilm was in my purse, and God only knows where that is now."

Mac grunted, mentally kicking himself. "Guess I've lived alone too long. I should have remembered that women always carry purses. I should have looked for yours that night but…"

"Don't blame yourself, honey. You saved me and that was enough. We were lucky to have gotten away from there. We'll find it somehow, when we get out of here."

"Sure, honey. Anyway, Kai doesn't know we don't have the film, so I think we're safe for the time being. As long as there is any doubt in his mind as to its existence, I don't think he'll make his move. However, that doesn't help our present situation to any great degree. We're still trapped in this mausoleum."

Mac picked up the phone again, and when he had the housekeeper on the line, he ordered himself some breakfast, and asked for another tray for Kim as her's had become cold.

While he was doing this, Kim started looking around the room speculatively. She got off Mac's lap, folded the blanket and placed it beside him, and started circling around the room, examining the walls. Mac noticed her as he hung up the phone and watched her in amusement as she started tapping on the walls.

Not finding what she was apparently searching for, she drifted into the bedroom. The walls in this room were a series of panels. Mac followed her to the bedroom door and stood watching her. She started tapping on the wall behind the four-poster bed. "Would it be too presumptuous of me to ask what the hell you're doing?" Mac chuckled.

Kim was undaunted. Ignoring his amusement, she explained, "Houses as old as this one often have secret passages. It'll be just our luck that any passages in this house will be on the other side of the building...probably in the library or dining room. I doubt we'd be so lucky as to..." She stopped suddenly and tapped again on one of the ornate panels on the inside wall. "Wait a minute! This sounds promising," she gasped.

Mac laughed outright as he moved toward where she stood, feeling around the panel with her small, graceful hands. "Come on, Sherlock, you've been seeing too many horror movies. Cut out all the sleuthing and come over here and give me a kiss."

"Mac, be serious," she countered. "It does sound hollow. Come and see."

Mac grabbed her playfully, and threw her on the big bed, tickling her until she was laughing so hard her stomach ached. She wrestled as well as she could, being weak from laughter, while he covered her neck and face with little quick kisses.

"I know something that really is hollow at the moment, and I'd love to volunteer to fill it up." he quipped.

All thought of secret panels momentarily forgotten, Mac proceeded to do exactly that, his heart beating hard against his chest as he eagerly filled her warm, inviting "hollow" with his impatient manhood.

When they had sated their desire, a strange feeling of peace seemed to come over them. He held her tenderly, as if she were a child, and she snuggled close to him, comforted by his masculine strength and warmth.

Without looking at his face, Kim asked in a small voice. "What if we don't get out of this, Mac? What if this is our last time together?"

Though she was voicing his own fear, he bluffed, "Nonsense, honey. We're going to get out—and soon. And, when we do, I'm rushing you to the nearest Justice of the Peace. I'm not taking any more chances on losing you."

She sat up quickly, looking at him in wide-eyed joy. "Oh Mac, darling. Do you really mean it? After all, you've had to go through so much on my account. You really want to marry me?"

"More than you'll ever know, baby." He kissed her again, but this time it was a long, lingering, tender kiss that seemed to touch the bottom of his soul. Slowly he began to caress her. Lovingly his fingers worshiped her face and then trailed lightly down her neck. His arms slipped gently around her and they stood almost as one body. She relaxed into a security she had never known. Their lovemaking was slow, tender, and so exquisitely mutual in every way that they reached a peak that could only be described as spiritual. As they drifted back, they slipped into a deep and healing sleep, completely sated in their mutual passion and love.

Kai sat at his carved desk, a cigarette dangling from his thin lips. He watched Kato, as that inscrutable character made a pot of tea, generously spicing it with Jamaican rum. Kai often wondered about this sidekick of his. Seeing this man handling this small domestic task with such ease, it was hard to remember the cat-like quickness and total uninvolved way he could slit a man from belly to throat without a blink of an eye. Kai considered himself to be quite cool, but Kato… Now here was a definite enigma. Here was a man without one single known human emotion. Kai had to admit that Kato even scared him at times. Suffice it to say, Kai was glad to have Kato for an ally.

Kato brought the steaming, rummed tea and placed it before Kai, then sat across the desk from him, giving his total attention to the hot brew.

"Aren't you interested in the fate of our house guests?" Kai ventured. Kato peered at him over the rim of the teacup, but said nothing.

"Your usual eager anticipation, I see." Kai laughed his hard chuckle. "Were your men able to find anything?"

Kato took his time answering, enjoying a long sip of his tea. Finally, he looked up. "It wasn't in the alley."

Kai's eyebrows raised. "No? Well, I'm not really surprised. That means either Neely was lying, or the cops got it."

"What about that bartender? Do you think he has it somewhere? Or…maybe he gave it to the FBI already." Kato hissed.

"That's possible, of course, but if I read Neely right, he could be stalling for time. Of course, if the FBI does have it, that will make it a little uncomfortable for us."

Kato stared at him blankly. "If that's the case, we'd better make plans to move our operations back to Asia. Why don't you let me use a little persuasion on him? We don't know how damning the evidence against us might be."

"There isn't any evidence against us as long as we have Kim. They can't trace the gun to us. It was one we smuggled in from Taiwan. No, we won't make any move until I find out what the FBI has. I have a man in there who can dig up the information we need in the next couple of days. In the meantime, we'll wait."

An evil look flickered in Kato's narrow eye slits. "And when do I get my chance with the bartender and Kim?" Kato asked. "I'm getting very impatient, and you know how I get when I'm impatient," Kato said threateningly.

"I assure you," Kai said. "You will have your day. Their fates are sealed whatever happens, and I will thoroughly enjoy turning them over to you. But for the time being, I'm enjoying my little game of cat and mouse." A smile creased his face. "It is most fascinating, knowing Kim as I do, to watch their little love affair."

He held out his cup for Kato to refill. "Shall we call it 'research'?" He threw back his head and laughed, a sound so cruel in its intent that it would have curled the hair of any normal human being. Kato just stared, the usual immobility of his taught features not indicating the pleasure he allowed himself to feel as he took Kai's cup to refill it.

Mac lay still for a long time after he awoke. Kim was still snuggled in the curve of his arm, and he didn't want to disturb her. He also appreciated the time to think—to make plans. He had to do something to get them out of this house and out of Kai's clutches, and he would have to act fast. He didn't trust their snake-like host to leave them hanging around in his way for too much longer.

If only he had some kind of a weapon. His thoughts were getting him too excited now to stay in bed a moment longer, so he gently and slowly eased his arm out from under Kim's warm, yielding body, anxious not to awaken her. He got up quietly and started looking around the room for something to use as a weapon.

He found nothing of any use in the bedroom, so he systematically inspected the rest of the suite. Kai was too clever. There was not a nick-knack of any size and weight, and clocks and other large objects were firmly attached to their stands or shelves.

Discouraged, Mac went to the bar and fixed himself a Gin and Tonic. As he dropped a couple of ice cubes into the glass, a thought struck him. Ice cubes! Frozen water was a pretty hard substance. He quickly scooped up a couple of handfuls of ice and wrapped them in the center of a handkerchief; then he tied the ends of the hankie in a manner that left him enough to hold on to it firmly. This homemade club he tested by slamming it against his free hand, and discovered it had sufficient wallop to do the job. He slipped his handmade weapon into the freezer behind the bar for handy access when he should need it.

The next problem was going to be how to get the guard into the room. The housekeeper always delivered their meals; the guard stayed outside the door. If he could somehow attract the guard's attention and curiosity—somehow get him to open that door.... Mac racked his brain for an idea.

There was one possibility. It would all depend on the mental capacity of the guard, and whether he would take the initiative to act on his own or summon Kai and Kato. That was the gamble, but at this juncture, any kind of action, even if unsuccessful, was better than standing around worrying.

Mac decided to take the chance.

Unfortunately, it would involve Kim, but that couldn't be helped. Besides, she had to be ready to go as soon as the guard was out of the way anyway, so he went back into the bedroom and gently shook her awake.

She smiled up at him wistfully, but with such joy in her eyes that it took all his willpower not to take her in his arms again. "Come on, honey. We have to see what we can do about getting out of this mausoleum."

"What are you going to do?" she gasped. "Oh, Mac, please don't take any chances."

"Not 'me' honey, 'us'! Just do as I say, and we may have a chance of getting out of this place."

The guard leaned against the wall outside the great doors—half asleep. He was bored, and he had already been on duty for an hour more than he was scheduled for. His stomach was growling, and all he could think of was a nice hot meal and a good night's sleep. Maybe not even alone, he chuckled. The new parlour maid was a real looker—and she had given him the eye when she passed him in the hall this morning. If only he could just sit down for a while. But then the boss was probably right in not having a chair handy, because he knew he would have been asleep hours ago had he not had to stay on his feet. At this late hour, it was an effort to stay awake standing on his feet.

He was yawning as if to confirm his thoughts, and for the hundredth time trying to get his eyes fully open, when he was jolted into alertness by the sound of yelling coming from inside the prisoners' suite. By damn, he thought, it sounded as if the guy was beating the woman—and it was becoming more frantic.

What should he do? If he left his post now and anything happened to the prisoners, Kai would have him killed. But, on the other hand, he couldn't just stand there and listen to the woman's screams. His brain, not speedy at best, worked sluggishly in his large skull, but he finally gave in to his urge to take the physical solution. He pulled out his key and quickly unlocked the door. The noise of the woman's squealing came from the bedroom. He had pushed the door open

and started toward the bedroom when Mac's ice cube Billy club, with all the force of Mac's well-developed arm muscles, descended on his head. He started to fall forward, but Mac caught him quickly so as to prevent the sound of the large body hitting the floor. Then he felt for and found the guard's gun, which had dropped out of his hand when he was hit. It was lodged under the big man's chest, but Mac managed to get it free. He stuck the gun in his pocket, as Kim joined him.

"Ready, honey?" Mac asked as he pocketed the guard's keyring.

"Ready. But...how are we going to get out of the house? They must have guards everywhere." was Kim's wide-eyed reply.

"There must be a back staircase down one of these halls. I doubt if Kai would have guards posted there, because he figures there's no way for us to get out of the suite. We'll have to be fast and quiet. In the meantime, let's put this character out of action for a while." Mac quickly used the strips of sheeting they had torn up to tie and gag the unconscious guard.

"I wish we hadn't had to make all that racket, though. There's always the chance that someone else on this floor could have heard it too. Well, we don't have time to worry about that now. Come on!" He grabbed her by the arm and they ran quickly out of the room, Mac closing the big doors behind them and locking the guard in the suite.

"Which way?" Kim whispered frantically.

Mac scanned the hallway. "Let's try down here," he whispered, and then took off down the hall at a run with Kim close at his heels.

"Bingo!" Mac breathed as he pushed open a heavy door at the end of the hall and found the staircase looming in front of them.

They ran lightly down the stairs to the first floor, and Mac tried the outside door only to find it locked.

"Can't say I'm surprised." He pulled out the keyring and tried them one by one. "Hell!" he rasped, "just our luck. None of these work in this damned door."

What now? There was still the inner door. Perhaps they could get out through the back of the house. Surely these keys had to belong to some locks.

Mac tried the inner door and found it unlocked. With Kim close behind him, he pushed the door open an inch or two, trying to be quiet as possible—hardly breathing. He closed it abruptly.

"What is it?" Kim asked.

"Kai," he replied in a whisper. "He's standing at the foot of the main staircase talking to a dignified-looking guy in a white coat. Looks like a doctor, or something."

"Let me look. I might know who it is." She moved to take his place at the door, but he held her back.

"Too risky. He might see the door open."

"Well, what do we do now?" Kim looked up at him urgently.

"The only way left seems to be down," he said, and propelled her down the stairs toward the basement. "There must be some way out of the basement."

Whatever Mac expected to see in the basement of this old Gothic mansion, he was not prepared for what actually met their eyes. Here was no cobweb, filled cellar with storage rooms and wine cellars. Neat corridors ran hospital-like between cement walls that were unbroken by windows with only an occasional door that Mac would hazard were made of solid steel. The halls were dimly lighted, and had the slightly antiseptic smell of a hospital. Mac looked at Kim, who was staring in amazement at the modern, sanitized facility before her.

"What is this, Mac? What is this place?"

"Beats me, pumpkin, but it sure doesn't look like anything you would expect to find in an old house like this. Dracula's den would have surprised me less. No time to speculate now, though.

"Let's see if we can find a way out of this dump."

Mac led the way down the corridor and was about to make a turn at the first juncture when he suddenly jumped back, pressing Kim against the wall with his arm.

"Shhhh," he hissed.

"What is it?" Kim gulped.

"Shhhh," Mac warned.

Slowly Mac inched into a position where he could just see the hallway around the bend where Kai and the dignified man in the lab coat from upstairs entered the corridor and went to a large steel door. They stopped in front of it for a while and continued their conversation. Mac wished he could hear what they were saying, but they were too far away, and talking very intently in hushed tones.

After a second or two the man in the lab coat nodded, and Kai took a small device from his pocket and held it in his hand in front of the door. A small but intense beam of light ushered forth from it and hit the lock panel of the door. The door swung quietly open and the man in white entered. Kai flipped the bolt and locked the door again, then after looking up and down the corridor—as if by habit—he turned and started back upstairs by the front basement stairs.

When Mac was sure Kai was gone, he motioned to Kim to remain where she was, then slowly moved toward the steel door where the man had disappeared. When he reached it, he put his ear to the door, but quickly realized it was a useless gesture. He figured the door must be a good 6 inches thick. That, combined with the cement walls, made hearing anything from inside a sheer impossibility.

Mac turned and bumped into something soft. His heart jumped out of his chest. "Oh, Christ!" he rasped. "What the hell are you trying to do, give me a heart attack?" he hissed at Kim, who had followed him, and had been looking over his shoulder. She was staring at him with unconcealed anxiety.

"What is it, Mac? Could you hear anything? What did you see, anyway?" she cried.

Mac automatically hushed her, even though the cellar seemed to be pretty soundproof. He led her back down the hall and around the corner to where they had watched Kai and the man in white. He didn't want to take the chance of the man coming out of the room suddenly and finding them there.

"The man I told you about—the one that was talking to Kai in the front foyer—he's in that room. Kai locked him in, but he seemed to be here of his own free will. Some sidekick of Kai's, I guess, but he just didn't look the type. He looked like a doctor or a scientist, or something. Kai used some kind of a device to unlock the door—I'd say it was a laser beam."

"Laser beam? This is all crazy! It doesn't make any sense at all—this place, and now this man? What's Kai up to?" she wondered.

"I don't have the slightest idea, but it's becoming more mysterious every minute." "What do we do now, Mac?" Kim asked.

"Just what we were doing. Try to find a way out of here." They went down each hallway, until they realized they were going over the same territory. Much to their chagrin, they found no doors at all on the outside wall of the building. All told, there were four doors. Two solid steel leading to the interior rooms, and the two doors leading to the front and back staircases leading up into the house.

They couldn't hide their disappointment. Mac took Kim's hand and spoke softly, encouragingly. "We'll go back upstairs. There must be a door out of here somewhere, and we're going to find it."

Kim followed him, trying to be brave, and they started up the stairs which they had descended earlier. They were on the last few steps to the first-floor landing when the door above them flew open and Kato and the guard who they had left tied up in their suite stormed into the stairwell and started toward them, menacingly.

Mac and Kim stopped their ascent and turned quickly, starting to run down the stairs again. Kato shouted for them to stop, and Mac reached for the gun in his pocket. At that moment they reached the basement landing, and Mac pushed open the heavy door only to be greeted by the smiling face of Kai Ching and the cold steel muzzle of a handgun.

CHAPTER

Eleven

Mac's shoulders slumped as he begrudgingly dropped the gun into Kai's waiting palm.

"Oh, Mac" wailed Kim. Mac put his arm around her and held her close to his side, as they preceded Kai, Kato and the fuming guard up the wide staircase and were once again ensconced in their velvet prison. Kai entered with them.

"I hear you're an excellent bartender, Mr. Neely. Why don't you give me a sample? I haven't had a good Martini in a long time. Quite dry, if you please." Kai said in his most genial manner as he sank down into an easy chair near the bar.

"Be happy to oblige," Mac smiled, "only I'm missing the most important ingredient."

"Oh, I'm sorry. I thought I had been a most thorough host. What is it you need?" Kai questioned.

"A little Arsenic would be quite nice," Mac replied.

"You know, I'm rather disappointed in you, Mr. Neely."

"Why be formal after all we've been through together. Call me Mac. All my best enemies do!"

"Mac, then. I would really have thought you to be a better sport than this. You didn't really think it would be that easy, did you? No reason to get pouty about it. You really did a lot better than I thought you would. Quite clever, the ice bit. Too bad it was wasted. Oh, well. We can't as they say, win them all. Take it like a man, old boy. Take it like a man!"

That snaky smile again! At that moment, Mac could cheerfully have grabbed a hammer and smashed that pretty face into a pulp. Instead, he mirrored the smile, and finishing the martini he had been mixing behind the bar, he handed it to Kai.

"Your martini, Mr. Ching."

"Thank you, Mac. And you, of course, may feel free to call me Kai."

Kai settled himself further into the ornate easy chair and sipped his martini. "Mmmm. The rumors were right. Excellent! Don't think I've ever had a better martini, and I've had one in about every city in the world. My compliments, Mac." He sipped the martini slowly. "Oh, but you aren't going to let me drink alone, are you, Kim, my dear. You must have a Margarita. It's still your favorite, isn't it?" Kim nodded, looking at him with disgust in her lovely almond eyes.

"Fix the lady a Margarita, Mac, and of course fix yourself anything you like. My house is your house," he chuckled.

Mac handed Kim a Margarita and started fixing himself a whisky sour. Kim absently sipped her Margarita, and watched Kai to see how long this friendly super-host act was going to last. She knew him too well to suppose he was not hiding a festering anger that was bound to come out sooner or later. As she watched him, she noticed the gleam of an object on a silver chain around Kai's neck. She maneuvered around in her chair so that she could get a better look at it, and saw that it was an odd-shaped device that looked something like a small flashlight.

She looked up at Mac and indicated it with her eyes. He spotted it too, and realized it was the same device Kai had used to unlock the heavy metal doors in the basement—the laser device. If he could only get his hands on that device....

Kim figured it was worth a try, so she rose from her chair and went to sit on the arm of Kai's easy chair. Mac, taking her cue, addressed Kai.

"You don't mind if I go to the John do you, 'old fellow'?"

Kai looked up at Kim, his curiosity at what she was up to get the best of him, and replied, without looking at Mac, "Of course not, old man. Nature does have her priorities."

Mac, though hesitant to leave Kim alone with this madman, went through the bedroom door on his way to the bathroom. He closed the bedroom door behind him, then audibly closed the door to the bathroom, without entering it. Then he slowly crept back to the bedroom door and did a little old-fashioned keyhole peeping-tomming. He was damned sure going to be close at hand in case Kim needed any assistance. He knelt down and put his eye to the hole, and relaxed as he realized it afforded him a clear view of Kim and Kai. He settled down to watch, wishing he could throw off the foreboding that was gnawing away at his vitals.

As soon as the bedroom door had closed behind Mac, Kim had slipped from the arm of the chair onto Kai's lap, gallantly hiding the revulsion she now felt for this man who had wreaked such havoc in her young life.

"What's this?" Kai smiled. "My little Kimmy's not missing her daddy-lover now, is she?"

She fought tensing up, and forced herself to cuddle up to Kai's body. She ran her fingertips over his cheek "You know there'll never be anyone quite like you in my life, don't you, daddy?" she purred. "I've missed you. No matter what I may have said when I left, love's not that easy to turn off. Not when you've been as close as we have."

Summoning up all the sex appeal she had, which was considerable, she arched toward him and placed her lips on his, waiting for his answering response. It finally came.

"Well, well, well. What do you know? You've improved. I guess a little new blood was what you needed." He kissed her then with growing passion, and she threw her arms tightly around his neck. Showering his face and neck with hot kisses, short sweet, passionate, and praying that she would not be detected, she managed to unclasp the chain about his neck. In order to keep his mind occupied, she let her left-hand slip down and massage his hardened manhood through his trousers, as she maneuvered the chain and the precious device into her right fist.

Kai, still kissing her, suddenly reached up and, grabbing her lowcut dress at the top, gave a sudden wrench and ripped the dress from top to bottom, exposing her firm young breasts to his eager mouth. The sudden revulsion she felt as his wet mouth explored her body, physically sickened her. She was afraid that if he went any further, she would vomit all over him.

She tried to pull away, but it only seemed to make him more eager. Besides, if she was not careful, if she showed how horrible this was to her, Mac would be rushing in to rescue her before they got what they desperately needed...the device that she now held clenched in her fist.

Kai chuckled as he picked her up in his arms and tossed her nearly nude body, practically completely exposed by the remnants of her dress, onto the floor in front of the bedroom door. He reached quickly across her body and turned the lock on the door, just as Mac reached for the knob, not giving a damn about the device in his rage at seeing his woman being violated.

"Damn!" he breathed as he realized the door was locked. He lost all sense of reason and started pounding furiously on the door, swearing at himself for having let this thing go too far. He should have made his move when he first realized Kai meant to take her, but he had waited that one moment too long.

Kai laughed, his passion spurred on by Kim's thrashing and biting, and by the sounds of helpless rage coming at him through the bedroom door. He held her down and entered her with cruel, painful thrusts. She screamed out her terror and disgust with every angry thrust, calling Mac's name with each piercing entry.

Mac, completely out of his head now, started throwing his body against the heavy door, but no matter how many times he smashed his bruised shoulder against it, it would not budge an inch.

When Kai had loosed his seed and was completely sated, he raised himself off Kim's now inert body, and zipped his now limp organ into the protective confines of his shorts and trousers.

Kim, all fight burned out of her, lay without moving, shame and despair causing the tears to escape her tightly shut eyes and slide down her cheeks to the carpet. She grasped the device tightly in her hand, and tried not to think of Mac on the other side of the door—knowing her disgrace. The pounding had stopped now, but she couldn't know that her lover was on a heap against the other side of the door, crying from the deepest part of his guts—his own guilt at his part in this horror too great to face.

Kim felt hot and flushed with the shame of what had taken place. She had not meant this to happen. She had felt sure she could handle Kai as she had so many times in the past. What would Mac think? How would he feel about her now?

Kai stood looking down at her with his enigmatic grin spreading wider on his handsome, cruel face. Her eyes flew open in disbelief when she heard him start to chuckle and then break into a hearty laugh.

"Well, my dear, the struggle was mildly interesting, but that is hardly what I would have called passion on your part. You are, after all, no better than you used to be. You really should give it up, my love. You're quite obsolete, you know. You never, in my opinion, performed quite up to standards, but you have definitely gone downhill." She cringed, trying to shut out Kai's cruel words. "It's fortunate, really, that I can do much better than you, now."

Kim looked up at him, hardly able to believe his cruel words. Just having him look at her exposed body repulsed her. She grabbed helplessly at what was left of her dress, trying to cover her nakedness.

"You don't have to do that, my dear," Kai sneered. "I'm leaving now. You might as well stay there and be ready for your new 'lover boy'. Though what he sees in you, I can't imagine." Kai started toward the door, unlocked it from the inside, then turned back to Kim.

"Oh, before I forget, my dear, I'll take the laser now." Kim sat up quickly, clutching the device to her breast.

"But...how?"

"You never were trained to be a pickpocket, love. You really are extremely awkward." He held out his hand, and she slowly raised her aching body from the floor, hobbled over to him, and dropped the device in his open palm, tears of disappointment and humiliation streaming down her anguished face.

"Yes, my love. All for nothing. But don't feel too bad, my little Kimmy. The device wouldn't have done you any good anyway. It takes a special combination of turns to make it work, and I am the only person living who knows what that combination is." He turned and started to open the door, then looked back at her with a smile. "Besides, you'll not get the chance to escape from this suite again, and even if you did get back to the basement you would still be out of luck. You see there are no outside doors in the basement." He started out the door, and Kim, remembering Mac still locked in the bedroom, let out a little yip. Kai stopped.

"Oh, of course. How thoughtless of me. Your lover." He pulled a key from his trouser pocket and dropped it into her hand.

"I guess you might consider it a fair trade. But I always have been a soft touch, and young love is so appealing." He laughed shrilly as he closed the door locking it behind him.

Kim thought the sound of that laughter would haunt her to her dying day. So diabolical was the sound of it—and so damned triumphant.

Kim looked down at the key in her hand. She couldn't face the thought of Mac's eyes looking at her bruised and degraded body—not after what they had had together. She sank down on the carpet and the tears came afresh, torn from her sense of shame, as well as the futility that it had all been in vain. Her sobs rose to near hysteria, blotting out the sound of Mac's voice as he called to her, urging her to let him out. He continued to bang frantically on the door, calling her name.

Finally, his calls penetrated her benumbed brain and she struggled up, inserted the key in the door, and stood back, as Mac pushed his way into the room. He stopped as he saw her standing, clutching the remnants of her dress to her breast, her beautiful eyes swollen and downcast.

He moved to her slowly, murmuring her name softly, soothing her with his words as one would attempt to approach a wounded animal. When he reached her, he pulled her gently into his arms, reassuring her of his love, his support. She stiffened at first, then relaxed into his embrace, sobbing quietly now, her head on his shoulder.

He held her like that for a long time, noticing how very cold she was. He never knew anyone who could feel so cold. Finally, her sobs subsided and she lay limp against him.

Without a word, he carried her into the bathroom, ran a warm bath, added some scented bubble-bath that he found in the cabinet, and gently lifted her into the tub. Then he proceeded to gently bathe her and wash her hair, all the time reassuring her of his love and understanding.

"It's going to be fine, honey. It doesn't matter about the device. We'll find a way. All that matters is that you were wonderful, and brave, and I love you more now than ever before."

He gently patted her sweet young body dry with a large, soft towel, and then carried her to the bed and placed her gently on the sheets, covering her with the downy blankets.

"There never was a braver lady in the whole world." He kissed her cold lips. "Now you just rest, honey. Try not to think about it. It's over, and I'll kill him if he ever comes near you again. Just think about us, and how it's gonna be when we get out of this hole."

He tucked the covers in around her and she looked up at him, as if seeing him for the first time. She gave him a faint smile.

"I'll be all right, honey. It's okay. Don't worry. Only I'm cold. So very cold."

Mac quickly slipped out of his clothes and crawled in beside her. He pulled her chilled body close against the length of him, warming her by the strength of his will.

"Oh, Mac," she moaned. "I didn't get it. He knew I'd taken it and I had to give it back. Our only hope." She started weeping quietly.

"Honey, no. Don't," he soothed her. "We'll find another way. Only you must rest now. We're still alive and we're together. Close your mind to everything else but that, and try to get some sleep. It's almost 4 AM. It'll be getting light soon, and we'll want to be fresh to make some new plans."

She pressed herself up closer to Mac's reassuringly warm body. "Oh, Mac. It's so hopeless. Kai's so clever—and he's ruthless. He'll never let us get away. He'll play cat and mouse with us till he's bored, then...."

"No sweetheart, it's not hopeless. No one is perfect, not even Kai. There's got to be something he's overlooked, and it's up to me to figure out what that something is and use it to get us out of here."

At this, Kim rallied a little. "Us, honey. It's up to 'US'."

"Right. I stand corrected. Or, lay down corrected, whatever the case may be." They both chuckled, having the resilience of the young, and Kim, cuddled against her lover, soon gave in to her exhaustion, and was fast asleep.

However, there was no sleep for Mac. He laid there for a long time until he was sure she was deeply asleep, then slowly moved away from her and slipped out of the bed, putting on his bathrobe in the chill air.

He tried not to look at the spot on the other side of the open bedroom door where Kai had!!... He couldn't even voice it in his thoughts. The muscles in his jaw tightened as he gritted his teeth. He pulled on his trousers and got out a cigarette. Sitting on the edge of the bed, he racked his brain for a solution. He had a feeling they were running out of time.

~

Lt. Lindham hung the phone up with a loud bang. "What the hell do we pay these agents for?!" He picked up the receiver again and pushed the intercom button. Much to his secretary's chagrin, he yelled into the phone, "Get Stoner in here! Now!"

Todd Stoner, a burly, but agile, young man of about 25 sauntered in about a half-hour later. By this time, Lindham was pacing the floor like a caged animal. He swung around and opened his mouth to yell, when Stoner raised his hand protectively in front of his face and grinned. "Hey! I'm on your side, remember? Friends." Stoner smiled.

"Well, you sure as hell wouldn't know it. Where have you been?" Lindham snapped.

"Out doing your job for you," Stoner replied. "I hear you lost a couple of young citizens a couple days ago."

"Witnesses in the Ching case, damn it. I don't know how we slipped up. My man claims he got stuck in an elevator, and by the time he was back on Neely's trail, Ching's man had grabbed him. He saw the car driving away, but was on foot, so he reported back here... and there you are. A Royal fuckup. He stayed on the apartment, but nothing. The girl's gone too. Greer's fit to be tied."

Stoner smiled again—a Cheshire Cat grin, and sat on the edge of Lindham's doodle-carved desktop. "Well, you can both relax. We know where they are. What would you Feds do without us, local cops? Tsk, tsk, tsk." He shook his head in mock scolding.

Lindham's mouth fell open, and he dropped into his chair behind the desk. "You located them?! But, how...where...?"

"Don't look so surprised, Hal. The NYPD has a fairly good reputation, too, you know. I'd venture to say we could give Scotland Yard a run for their money any day."

"Sure, sure," Lindham acquiesced, "but why those two. How?..... This was a top-secret deal."

"Well," explained Stoner, "you know we've been after Ching and his gang, too. We've had his henchmen covered for about a month now. Knew every move they made. This time we just happened to be a step ahead of you." He grinned, mighty pleased with himself, then turned serious. "One problem though. Even though we know where they're being held, I'm afraid it will be next to impossible to get them out. And, if I know Ching, they're on a very short string. He gets bored with new toys quickly. We may not be able to get to them in time."

Lindham's relief at the news Stoner had imparted was very short-lived. The frown lines on his broad forehead deepened leaving him looking about 10 years older. "We have to. There's more at stake than meets the eye. Something really strange is going on with Ching's operation. The reports we have don't make much sense, but I can tell you this, whatever Ching is up to it's big! And dirty. I want those two young people out of this—now—before they get any more involved."

Stoner sat down on the chair across from Lindham. "Okay, let's get cracking. What do you want us to do?"

CHAPTER Twelve

Kim was, blessedly, still asleep, but Mac had been pacing the floor for hours with a drink in his hand, wracking his brain and coming up blank. He finally took a sip of his drink only to make a face. The ice had melted, and the drink was warm and watery.

He finally collapsed on the front room couch, sat the drink on the coffee table, and buried his face in his hands, his posture mirroring his despair.

The sound of the rain on the windowpanes, plus his general fatigue acted like a tranquilizer, and he didn't realize he had dozed off until something woke him with a start. A sound, sharp and close at hand. No…a series of sharp sounds…taps…short, sharp taps.

He rubbed his eyes with his hands, trying to regain his alertness. Must have been his imagination, he decided.

No. There it was again. That same sharp, tapping—almost like some kind of a code. It came from the large window which was heavily draped against the cold night air. He cautiously moved to the window and pulled aside the drapes. It was hard to see anything because of the thick wrought-iron bars and the heavy rain streaming down the panes. He waited, holding his breath. The taps sounded again, and he could make out the outline of a fist as it hit the glass.

He reached over and tapped on his side of the pane. Then waited. A second or so later, a blurred face was pushed up against the outside of the pane, rivulets of water obscuring the features.

This didn't make sense, but Mac knew it couldn't be one of Kai's men. They would have no reason to be knocking on his window in the rain, so he felt around for the window lock then, finding it, loosened it with great effort. He then pushed the window up about a foot from the bottom. It moved hard but thank God it had moved. He breathed a thank you that the window had not been nailed shut.

Some masculine grunts preceded a broad, rain-drenched face up to the bars. The man grinned broadly, water dripping from his chin. Mac couldn't help but return the grin.

"I'm Todd Stoner. Lt. Stoner of the NYPD. Are you and the lady, all right?"

Mac's heart seemed to leap into his throat, and he could hardly reply. "Oh, thank God! How did you find us? Does Lindham know where we are?"

Todd grinned, "He didn't till I told him. I've been planted here as a gardener for around two months now, to keep an eye on whatever it is that Ching is hatching in this old mansion. When I saw them bring you two in, I contacted Lindham. I told him we knew where you were, and he brought us up to date on you and Ms. Henry." He made an effort to frame his eyes, so the rain would not keep him from seeing. It was a stinging, hard rain—almost on the verge of being hail.

"I wish I could let you in, but…" Mac commiserated with Stoner, indicating the intimidating bars.

"Oh, don't worry about that. One of the hazards of war. I don't mind…just glad to be able to communicate with you."

"Well, when and how do you get us out of here?" Mac asked, feeling almost lighthearted at this turn of events.

"We don't, sorry to say," came Stoner's reply.

"You don't!?? Did I hear you right? Man, don't you know they're planning to kill us?"

"Not if we can help it…but there's no way to get you out of the house right now. We can't tip our hand till we have some hard evidence to convict Ching and his people. I've been trying to get at his safe, but it's too well guarded day and night. We want to get you out as quick as possible, but we need your cooperation to help us get some hard proof of what's going on in this place."

"Evidence?" Mac hissed. "You'd take a chance on our lives for some damned evidence?"

"Take it easy, Neely. I know how you must feel, but..."

"You know how I feel? How the hell can you. If you had seen what that animal did to my woman, you'd...you'd..."

"Easy, Neely. We will get you out, but it's not going to be easy. This place is practically escape-proof. Ching planned it well. The old dump is just like the Bastille."

"What the hell are we going to do? There must be some way out! There has to be."

"We're working on it, but as I said, in the meantime we need to get hold of something that will incriminate Ching."

Mac tried to hide his disappointment. Then he remembered Kim's dossier. "But there is proof! Microfilm of a dossier plus photographs of documents that could put Kai away for life. We don't have to get in the safe!"

"A dossier?! Fantastic! Where is it, for God's sake?" Stoner rasped.

"It may be lost," Mac admitted dejectedly.

"Lost?"

"Yes. You see it was in Kim's purse the night she was attacked by Kai's henchman. I left it in the alley in my haste to get away, and get Kim to safety. God only knows what's happened to it, but you could do a search of that alley. By some miracle it might show up."

"I'll get someone on it right away, but, in the meantime, I was able to get hold of a floorplan of the house. An old one, of course—minus Ching's changes." He pulled a soggy hankie from his soaked jacket pocket and wiped at the rain streaming down his face. "It does show something surprising though, well...may not so surprising, knowing the age of this place." He fumbled in his trouser pocket and came up with a plastic rolled bundle and handed it through the bars to Mac, who grabbed it eagerly.

Mac fumbled with the wrapping, all thumbs in his excitement. He unrolled the floorplan, flattening it out on the floor near the window.

"As you can see, there's a secret passage marked on there. It looks like it might open up into that room over there." Stoner motioned with his rain-soaked head toward the bedroom where Kim was still sleeping peacefully. "If so, and if it's still usable, you might be able to get down to the basement. There is only one door that I have been able to find which leads from the basement directly into the garden. It's been sealed up from the inside, but I think if we worked on it from both sides, we might be able to get it open."

Mac scrutinized the map carefully, scratching his head. "Well, I'll be damned. Kim was right. There is a passage. That blows my mind!"

Stoner moved cautiously to get a more comfortable foothold. "Look, I can't stay here much longer. The rain is good cover, but it's slowing down a bit now, and these people are pretty damned cautious. See what you can find out about the passage and if it's going to be of any help. I may not be able to contact you again, but if you find you can get down to the basement, be there a little after 3 am. Knock on the inside of the sealed door, if you can locate it. I'll be on the outside, and we'll work together on getting you two out of this hell-hole." Stoner turned to adjust his position for the climb down the side of the building, then stopped and leaned in to Mac again. "And, if you can get into the library some way—maybe by that passageway—see if you can get at that safe. If that other dossier is lost, we'll need anything Ms. Henry can lay her hands on. They're up to something, and it's big—international—bigger than dope even. We have to find out what it is." His face was anxious, and Mac nodded to reassure him.

"Don't worry, we'll do all we can...and thanks! You don't know what a relief it is just to know somebody is with us."

Stoner smiled a soggy smile and moved away from the window into the downpour. Mac lowered and locked the window, then went to the bar and grabbed a bar towel. He wiped up the rainwater that had splattered on the sill and tried to soak up enough of the water from the rug so that it wouldn't be too noticeable. Then he closed the heavy drapes and collapsed onto the couch. He breathed a deep sigh of relief and felt more relaxed than he had in the last few days—although he was filled with an inner excitement and anticipation. At least now there was some action to take—something to do to ease the frustration of being a helpless victim.

His thoughts were interrupted by the housekeeper bringing their dinner, which he accepted with a polite "thank you."

He carried the tray of steaming food into the bedroom where Kim was still sleeping peacefully, her body once again satisfied by the drug. He hated to wake her and bring her back to reality, but...they had to eat. They had a job to do this night.

He sat the tray down on the bedside table and reached out and touched her silky hair, then ran his hand over her warm cheek. She opened her eyes, saw it was him, and smiled up into his eyes.

The meal was delicious, as usual, their jailer having a gourmet taste. They hadn't had a bite to eat since noon and with all the excitement of the near escape, they were both ravenous. Their appetite for food finally sated, they snuggled a little, and before it could turn into anything too heavy, Mac held her away from him and looked into her eyes. "Do you know, I think you must be one of those ESP people...psychic or something."

"Why? What do you mean?" she queried.

"I'll show you." He got up and went to the wall panel she had been tapping on that morning. He tapped a few times, remembering where the map had placed the door, and was pleased with the hollow sound he produced on the last few taps. He ran his hands over the filigree work on the panel looking for some kind of release button.

"What on earth are you doing?" Kim asked, coming up beside him.

"Looking for your damned secret panel," was his reply, as he pulled the house plan out of his pocket again to see if there was any clue to opening the panel, once located.

"What's that? Where did you get that!?"

Mac smiled, then had to laugh at the amazed look on her face. He quickly told her of the visit by the police lieutenant. She stood open mouthed while he completed his story, then flew at him, hitting him in the chest with both of her small fists.

"What!? There was a policeman right out there and you let me sleep?!! You beast!

"You no good..."

Mac burst out laughing as he held her off, her fists missing his chest by a good six inches. "Now, now, honey! Control yourself. Temper, temper! He swung her around and got her in a gentle stranglehold, then his mouth came down on hers in a playful kiss which quickly smoldered into a passion. He pulled away reluctantly, gently releasing his hold on her. He gulped in a great breath of air and mentally told his aroused organ to cool it. There was no time for exercising that particular set of muscles now. "Now, if you'll let me get back to my work..."

Kim smiled, and her eyes lowered till her gaze was on the large bulge in his trousers. "But...he wants to play, honey." she smiled alluringly up at him.

"Well, he'll just have to wait. Work now, play later. Now, there has to be a release here somewhere..."

Kim sighed, then reached over and gave his manhood a pat, and directed her words to it. "Well, sweet one, we'll have to take a raincheck for now, I guess."

Mac laughed and patted her butt. "Get to work, woman! Help me look!"

It was Kim who finally found the latch after a ten-minute search. To their satisfaction, the panel moved smoothly and opened noiselessly, in spite of the fact that it probably hadn't been used in years. This was attested to by the myriad of cobwebs that clung to the inside of the passageway. She could not contain a smug look at Mac, and he teasingly forbids her to say, "I told you so."

Mac stepped gingerly into the opening, but Kim reached out and pulled him back. "Honey, wait. It's pitch black in there. What are we going to use as a light? I'm not going in there without a candle, or something. God knows what kind of creatures may be down there."

"You're not going there at all. I am," Mac stated flatly.

Kim let out a yelp. "Oh, no you're not. It's my passage and I'm going too." She had such a deadly determined look on her lovely face, that Mac relented.

"Okay, but you're right. We'll have to rig up a light of some kind. Damn! If only I had my flashlight."

They thought in silence for a moment or two, then Kim smiled. "I know. Those fancy old candles on the living room mantle. The candlesticks are sealed down but the candles should come out."

They rushed into the living room of their ornate prison, and Mac grabbed a handful of the elaborate, and obviously very expensive candles and shoved them at Kim, who grabbed them eagerly. "Kai's sure not going to like this," he smiled. He grabbed a few for himself. "These have to be antiques. He'll fry."

"All the more reason for burning them," Kim smiled, an evil glint in her slightly Asian eyes.

Mac patted his pocket to make sure he had sufficient matches, then they rushed back to the open panel. They lighted two of the candles, and Mac shoved the rest of the candles in his jacket pocket. Then they stepped quietly into the dark, musky passageway, Mac in the lead, Kim following, reluctant to face the hazards of the unknown, but strangely excited, too.

At the end of a very short landing, they found the steps leading downward. Mac had hoped there might be steps going up to the roof, a possible means of escape, but to his disappointment, there were only stairs leading down into the mansion. They started slowly down the steps, the candle flames giving only a faint glow in the encircling darkness. Cobwebs brushed against their faces and entangled their silvery strands in Kim's long, free-flowing hair.

Suddenly Kim let out a yelp and threw herself into Mac's arms, almost making him drop his candle. "What is it, honey?" Mac urged.

"We have to be quiet!" Kim yelped. "Something brushed against my leg—something soft and warm."

He pulled her to him to comfort her and felt her genuine fear as her body trembled in his arms. "It was probably just a rat. This is a very old house," he comforted.

"Oh, gee, thanks," she murmured sarcastically. "That's a great comfort."

"They won't hurt you, pumpkin. The rat was probably more surprised and frightened than you were."

"Wanna bet?" Kim countered.

Mac gave her a quick hug and they continued slowly downward. Mac stopped suddenly, causing Kim to bump into him, so close was she sticking to his protective presence. "Hey, what's the idea?" she grumbled.

"Shhhh!" he cautioned. "I hear voices."

"Where the heck are we?" she whispered.

Mac tried to picture the floorplan in his mind. "I think we're somewhere near the library, maybe behind the fireplace. The floorplan showed an exit into the library through the fireplace. Wait a minute. These passage entries usually have peepholes or something—there should be one on this inner wall." He poked around for a second, and was rewarded by finding a small circle that was hinged to swing to the side. He slowly and quietly worked at it to loosen the dirt and rust that had formed around the edges. Finally, it moved aside to reveal a small, but sufficient peephole. The voices were louder now, and he cautioned Kim not to make a sound.

Putting his eye up to the peephole he was able to make out the back of Kai's blond head as he sat at his high desk. Kato's evil face was in view as he stood in front of the desk, listening to his lord and master.

"You must check the guard every so often," Kai urged. "Change them every four hours so they'll be alert. I don't like leaving you alone here tonight, but this business is extremely urgent. We have to get more raw materials for Dr. Bronstein. Oh, and he'll be working in the lab again tonight so see that he's not disturbed."

Kato nodded his agreement, then asked, "Will you be back in the morning?"

"Yes. Quite late though, I'm afraid." Kai lamented. "I'm trusting you to see that our "guests" are well attended to. And don't look so disappointed. You'll have them soon enough. Right now, they're more valuable to us alive, but their usefulness is quickly running out and they'll be all yours." His evil laugh rang out and Mac could see a perverted look of pleasure on Kato's ugly face. Mac shivered in spite of himself, and Kim prodded him, impatient to look through the peephole herself. He shook his head for her to wait a while and listened as Kai continued.

"I must say, it amuses me beyond measure to watch that idiot fawning over Kim. I can't wait to see his face when our little secret is revealed, can you, my friend?" Kato's winged eyebrows lifted in appreciation of his employer's humor. "You may go now, Kato. I'll be leaving in a few minutes."

As Kato slithered out of the room, Kai got up, picked up some papers from his desk, and carried them to a portrait of Henry the Eighth, which he moved aside to reveal a small wall safe. Mac swore under his breath, and Kim poked him. "What's going on?? What's he doing? Here, let me see!" She pushed at him to make him move. Mac shushed her, trying to see the combination but it was just too far away for his 20-20 vision. He sighed, as he quietly closed the peephole cover.

"Come on Mac," she pleaded. "What's happening?"

Mac placed his hand over her mouth gently and whispered, "I'll tell you in a minute. Follow me."

She looked anxiously at the closed peephole, sorely tempted to open it, but Mac pulled her by the arm, and they slipped quietly down the remaining steps to the basement.

When they reached the bottom landing, Kim held the two candles while Mac searched the walls of the small passageway for an exit into the basement. When he finally found the latch, his heart sank. It was covered with rust and totally immovable. The more he worked at the latch with his bare hands, the more discouraged he got. It simply wouldn't budge. He stood up and looked at Kim, beautiful in the candle glow. She stared back at him, her large brown eyes full of questions.

"Can't budge it, pumpkin. We'll have to come back later and bring some kind of tool to loosen the rust." She looked very downhearted and discouraged so he put his arm around her slim shoulders. "It's okay, honey. We'll get it open. Let's get back upstairs now though, before somebody starts checking up on us."

Kim yelped. "Oh, I hadn't even thought about that! Let's go."

He started up the stairs again as quietly as possible, Kim closely behind him, trying not to give in to the near hysteria she was feeling inside. She felt a sense of great relief as they stepped out of the dusky passage into the warm and reassuring bedroom.

"Never thought I'd be glad to see this room," she sighed. "I'm going to take a shower. I'm covered with dust and cobwebs, and Lord knows what else." She looked up from brushing dust from her skirt and saw him looking at her with love in his eyes. "Wanna join me?" she teased.

"You don't have to ask twice," he chuckled, climbing quickly out of his smutty clothes. He felt his manhood harden as he watched her undress, the dress being thrown on a chair and the delicate undergarments dropping at her feet. Her young, lithe body was full of youthful vitality, her full breasts taut in anticipation, the nipples hard and full.

She threw her panties at him, and they hit him in the chest. He tossed them aside as she sprinted for the bathroom. He caught up with her as she was adjusting the water temperature, and lifted her off her feet, carrying her into the stall with him, feeling the thrill of his manhood pressed against her rounded buttocks. The hot water beat down on their naked bodies as they stood entwined, their lips, torsos, and hips pressed tightly together, arms and legs entwined, and not all the steam came from the hot water. He entered her standing there, and their passion flamed to a crescendo. Their excitement and delight were total.

Afterwards, he dried her all over with a large, fluffy towel and she returned the compliment. He wrapped the towel around his loins, and as she went back into the bedroom to don a gown, he shaved. Just as he finished, he felt a tug, and the towel disappeared from around his waist. She giggled playfully as he chased her around the apartment, grabbing at the towel as she played matador. He caught up with her in the living room and threw her down on the couch, wrestling with her for the towel. They both jumped when a knock sounded at the door. Mac looked up and called, "Who is it?"

"The housekeeper, sir," was the unwelcome reply. "Is everything all right? I can bring you some coffee and toast, if you like."

Mac looked to Kim and she nodded. He had other appetizers on his mind, but he gave her a frown and called back to the housekeeper, "Yes, thank you, Mrs... Uh, that will be fine."

"Be right back!" the housekeeper called as they heard her steps disappear down the hall. Mac jumped up, wrapping the elusive towel around his waist, and moved to the door. He jiggled the handle, just in case, and was rewarded by a gruff-voiced growl from the guard, "You need something else?" sounding through the heavy door. "Uh... no thanks," Mac replied, moving back to the couch. "So, young lady. You'd rather eat toast than me, huh?" He swooped down on her and set her into a fit of the giggles.

They cuddled on the couch until the coffee came. When the housekeeper was safely away, they settled down to munching and discussing their next trip to the basement. "We'll wait until after midnight," Mac said. "We've got to figure out a way to loosen that latch. Hell! I wish we weren't so damned limited in things to work with. Thanks to Kai's rattrap mind, not a stone's been left unturned that might help our efforts."

"Yes, but Sherlock, you have forgotten one very important asset you have going for you." she smiled smugly.

"You mean this one?" He grabbed a handful of the soft flesh of her derriere and squeezed it gently, "I said ass-ette dear." she giggled.

"Oh, and what is that?"

"That little ole Dr. Watson—ME," her eyes twinkled.

"Okay, Watson. What's so elementary?"

She reached over and picked up the gleaming butter knife that rested among the crumbs and held it in front of his face. He caught her meaning and grinned. "A little dull, but I think it might just do the job."

"And..." said Kim. "I didn't save my butter patties to save calories." Her eyes twinkled, showing how pleased she was with herself.

"Right," Mac exclaimed. "The butter should loosen some of the rust, and I should be able to pry the rest away with the butter knife. You little Minx, what would I do without you?"

Unexpectedly, a cold shiver ran through Kim, almost like a premonition of evil, and she put her arms around his neck and whispered, "That's one thing I hope you'll never have to find out." Something about the way she looked, or the tone of her voice made Mac feel uneasy, too, so he pulled her closer to him and his lips found hers. It was a serious kiss, so unlike the earlier playful lovemaking, and it left them both with a strange, uneasy feeling.

Mac covered by elaborating his plans in detail. "I'll put the butter in the ice bucket to keep it cool and hard till we're ready to use it. Then at midnight or one o'clock, we'll go back down and try again. We can also see if there's a way to get into the library and see what Mr. Kai Ching has sequestered in that wall safe." He noticed that Kim's eyes were drooping, and her head came to rest on his shoulder. "It's 10:00 now. Let's get some shut-eye." She mumbled her agreement, and he smilingly lifted her in his arms and carried her into the bedroom where he placed her on the bed and covered her with the sheets and a light blanket. He crawled in beside her and sat watching her for a while as she slept. She was so very beautiful. It was hard for Mac to believe that this delicate, charming creature could really be his. There was something so different about her from any woman he had ever known. A quality, untiring zest for living. His heart was full as he cuddled up next to her, his arm protectively across her waist, and dropped off to sleep.

After the first deep slumber, Mac slept fitfully, afraid to drop off too deeply and miss their appointment with Kai's mysterious basement.

About 12:45, he looked at his watch for the 400th time, got up, and dressed quickly. He shook Kim awake, and as she dressed, he went into the living room and took the butter knife from the tray. He went to the cooler and got the patties of butter and put them in a small cup.

He held a few matches to it until the butter started to melt. He figured it would soften more as they made their way downstairs.

They only had four candles left, and Mac didn't know how long they would be in the darkness of the basement, so he fashioned a torch from some strips of pillow casing from their bed wrapped around the handle of a plunger he had discovered down underneath the cupboard in the bathroom. He opened a bottle of whiskey and slowly poured it over the tightly wrapped linen until the fabric was thoroughly soaked.

"How long do you think it will burn?" Kim asked, coming out of the bedroom and admiring his handiwork.

"It's pretty thick. With any luck at all, it should burn for about an hour. We'll use the candles first, so we'll have better light if we have too much trouble with the rusty latch." He grabbed a couple of books of matches from a bowl on the bar. "Well, baby. This is it! Let's go."

CHAPTER

Thirteen

The point of the knife dug deep in the rutted wall of Kato's quarters in the rear of the main floor behind the kitchen. Kai had let him cover one entire wall with wooden planks for his knife throwing practice. When he wasn't out doing Kai's dirty work, he spent his time in the small, stuffy room, throwing his knives with enviable precision.

Right now, he was restless and even more unhappy than was his usual wont. He couldn't understand why the boss was pampering these two prisoners so. He had always hated Kim. The whole idea was abhorrent to him, and gave him an eerie feeling that he didn't like. This scheme of Kai's was the wildest he had ever come across. Of course, he had to admit to himself that up until Kim had run away, it had been working very well—and bringing in unheard-of profits— which he, as the top man under Kai—shared in.

No, if he was honest with himself, he had nothing to complain about. Still...he got up and walked over to the knife, pulled it out of the wall, and because he needed something to do, he slipped the knife in his belt and, leaving his room, headed for the basement just to give it a look-see.

Kim quickly got dressed and followed Mac closely as they entered the dark passage once again and descended the dirt-encrusted stairs. When they reached the main floor, Mac snuffed the candles and opened the peephole. After the first few seconds of darkness, his eyes adjusted and he saw the shadows of the still-hot embers of the fire which had died down, playing on the inner sides of the fireplace. There was no one in the room. Not a sound could be heard except the occasional crackling of the dying embers in the fireplace and the beating of his heart in his ears.

He systematically started searching for the latch which would open the trap door at the rear of the fireplace. Kim joined him. A few minutes later, the door swung open, narrowly missing the embers which would have been scattered all over the rare oriental carpet.

Mac helped Kim over the embers and stepped over them himself, feeling the warmth against his feet and ankles. Kim had already stepped into the room, and as Mac followed, he looked to his right and spotted the painting of the Butcher King hanging above a short bookcase. Kim looked around, fearfully.

"Mac," she whispered. "We'll never find his safe. There must be at least 20 pictures on the walls, and dozens of cabinets." She looked very disheartened as Mac came up beside her.

"No problem, pumpkin," he returned in a whisper. "I know where it is." She looked at him surprised. "The peephole, remember?"

She sighed her understanding, and followed Mac as he led the way to the large, original painting of what looked like a royal personage of about the time of Queen Elizabeth I. As she gazed at the picture, something clicked in her head, and she knew that this must be the legendary Henry the Eighth. She didn't know quite how she knew, but the answer was just there in her brain. She shuddered a little as she gazed at this man, who had sacrificed so many women to his own greed for immortality.

By this time, Mac had reached the painting and was swinging it back, revealing the wall safe.

"Now what?" Kim queried. "I've never seen this type of safe before, and I don't have the combination to this one."

"Where do you suppose he might keep the combination?" Mac said, looking toward the hall door cautiously. "We don't have time to waste."

"If I know Kai, the combination is only in his head. But we can check around, maybe in the desk, or..."

Her whisper was interrupted by a distinct sound in the hall. She looked at Mac, fear in her eyes. He slammed the painting back in place and grabbed for Kim. She almost let out a yelp as she felt a sharp pain in her leg when he pulled her down beside him under the huge desk. He blew out the candles.

It was not a moment too soon, as the door opened silently, and Kato peered into the darkened room. Mac held his breath as the thought came to him that the trap door behind the fireplace was ajar. If Kato should notice it....

A second later they heard the door close and Kato's footsteps recede down the hall.

"My God, Mac," breathed Kim. "I thought he'd notice the trap door for sure."

Mac breathed deeply, "He would have but fortunately the embers have burned themselves out. If they'd still been burning?"

Mac pulled his matches out and relit two new candles, stuffing the stubs of the old candles in his jacket pocket. He held the candle up to his watch. 1:30! "We better forget about the safe for now. If we don't find that outside door soon, we'll miss Stoner." As he spoke, he helped Kim to her feet and they quietly, but quickly, stepped through the fireplace and back into the musty passageway.

When the trap door was securely closed behind them, Mac picked up the homemade torch he had left inside the passage, and they proceeded down the rickety stairs to the lower landing. Once there, Mac gave Kim the candles to hold and went to work on the rusty latch. He pulled the cup with the melted butter out of his inside jacket pocket, unwrapped the paper towels surrounding it, and dripped some of the butter on the latch. Then he pulled out the stainless-steel butter knife and set to work.

"Mac," Kim muttered. "What about those big steel doors in the basement? How will we get past them? If there is this outside, boarded up door, it has to be on the other side of those steel doors."

Mac grunted, trying to fit his big bulk into a more comfortable, workable position. "We'll just have to play it by ear, baby. One step at a time—or one latch at a time."

"Very funny!" Kim said, poking him in the ribs with her elbow.

"Watch it, pumpkin. You just dripped hot wax on my nose."

"Good," she parried. "If I drip enough on it, you'll look like Jimmy Durante. And I just love men with big noses."

He chuckled, then grunted as he chipped away at a particularly large deposit of rust. "More butter here, honey." She put both candles in her left hand and picking up the butter-filled cup, let some drip out on the obstinate latch.

For the next 15 minutes, she watched as Mac hacked away at the rust of who knows how many years. The candles were down to about two-inch stubs. "Better stop for a minute and light the torch. My hand is aching from trying to work with this damned little knife. My kingdom for a nice sharp chisel and a hammer." Kim held the candle stubs as Mac picked up the torch and held it near the candle flame. "Stay back from the torch as far as you can, honey," Mac warned. She pulled back and turned her face away just as the makeshift torch burst into flame. "Boy, that's a much better light, but I don't know how long it will last. Here, honey." Mac handed the torch to Kim, who blew out the candle stubs and held the torch down near the latch.

"Is it coming at all?" she asked.

"I think I've almost got it loose," Mac replied. "Yes, it's moving. There, I've got it!" His voice mirrored his excitement as the rusty latch, at last, gave way. Mac wiped the perspiration from his brow with his sleeve. "Whew, that was rough. But it should open now." He put his shoulder to the door and gave it a shove, expecting it to give way to his weight. Much to his disappointment, it didn't budge.

"What the hell!?" he swore.

"What's wrong, honey?"

"I'll be damned if I know. I can see the door is cracked. The lock is free and the door is moving, but..." He shoved against the door again, using all his considerable weight behind the effort. This time it moved slightly. "It feels like there's something big blocking the door on the other side."

"Here, let me help." She propped the burning torch in a crack in the floor, making sure it wasn't near the wooden walls, then, squeezing in next to Mac, put her shoulder to the door.

"Ready, now? Push!" Mac instructed. They threw their combined weight against the door and pushed. Nothing. Again, and again, they attacked the stubborn door, until finally their efforts were rewarded. The door moved slightly until it was open about three inches. Mac slipped his hand through the opening and felt about on the other side. "File cabinets. It must be a couple of big file cabinets. Full ones, by the feel of them. Come on, we can move them if we keep pushing."

Kim's shoulder ached and she felt like crying. Just as she was going to give up, the heavy files cleared an obstruction on the basement floor, jolted a little, and moved about a foot. It was just enough to let them squeeze through, and squeeze it was, but a few minutes later found them both, bruised and sweating, in the main hallway of the basement. Kim held the torch, which she had grabbed, out in front of them. All that faced them was the dark hallway with its strange medicinal odor. "Now what?" Kim asked.

Mac wiped his forehead with his hankie, his brow furrowed with his deep concentration. "First thing, I think we better push the door closed and move these files back against it. We can stick this matchbook in the lock so we can get back—if we have to, that is." He noticed the disappointment on her face at the thought of having to return to their velvet prison.

"Don't worry, pumpkin. I'm sure everything's going to go fine. Just leaving the way open as a safety precaution." She tried to smile, but it wasn't her best effort.

With Kim's help, they pushed the heavy files back into place. Mac marveled at the strength this tiny lady possessed. She was truly very special, and as they finished, he grabbed her and kissed her hard. "Just to let you know you're still my favorite lady."

She relaxed in his arms and the smile came easier now. "As long as we're together, I can handle anything," she whispered.

"The trick now is to figure out some way to get into that room we saw yesterday. It's on the right side of the house. The outside door has to lead from somewhere behind those steel doors."

"Don't you have any ideas?" Kim questioned.

"One," Mac answered. "When we were behind the fireplace this evening, I heard Kai say that a Dr... I think it was Bernstein or Bronstein, would be working in the laboratory tonight. I'm pretty sure that's the door we saw. If we can figure out some way to make him open the door from his side..."

"But how can we go in if this doctor's in there? He might be armed—anything!" Kim whimpered.

"That's the chance we have to take. I promised Stoner I'd find that door, if it still exists, before 3:30. That's his cover—his life, maybe—to help us get out of here. We have to do our part. Besides, it may be our only hope of getting out of this dump."

"What if he's not there? What if we find the door and he's not on the other side? What if he's already been caught? Oh, Mac, I'm so scared."

"Hey, come on now, my little worry-wart. Where's your positive thinking?" Mac soothed, as he gave her a quick hug. "We're gonna be just fine. Don't worry that beautiful head about it." She smiled and they moved quickly and quietly down the corridor toward the door to the laboratory.

"It smells awful down here," Kim interposed. "Like a hospital—or a morgue." She shivered. "What on earth could they be doing with a laboratory?"

"Too bad we didn't get that damned laser gadget." The moment he said it, he was sorry. He glanced quickly at Kim, and in the light from the torch, saw the pain of remembrance of her wasted sacrifice. "Sorry, pumpkin. That was thoughtless of me."

Mac jumped. "What is it?" Kim looked at him in alarm. "I think I heard something," Mac whispered. He grabbed the torch from Kim and dropped it onto the cement floor, stomping out the flames that were already diminishing as the sheets burned through. "Quick!" He pulled her back into the niche where the file cabinets stood, sorry he hadn't left the door to the passage ajar, as they heard heavy footsteps coming down the basement steps from the main house. They held their breath.

CHAPTER

Fourteen

Kato flashed the bright beam from his flashlight down the halls of the basement in a very peremptory manner. "Think I was a damned night watchman," he sneered. "Running around the house in the middle of the night! To hell with it! I'm gonna get drunk and go to sleep." If he had been a little less angry and a little more alert, he would have noticed the toes of Kim's high heel pumps sticking out from the alcove at the end of the hall, but as it was, he turned angrily and took the stairs up two at a time, his mouth watering in anticipation of the liquor he was going to filch from Kai's generous supplies in the library bar. He had found the key many weeks ago, and had a duplicate made. Since then, he had been helping himself liberally, always removing bottles from the back so his theft would not be noticed by Kai.

It was not that Kai would withhold liquor from his top henchman, but he did want to keep the man with a clear head, and knew that when he was drinking, he was almost impossible to manage.

The door slammed shut behind him and the basement was once again dark, except for a small yellow bulb that burned outside the laboratory door.

Mac and Kim breathed a sigh of relief. After a good ten minutes, Mac led the way back to the laboratory door. "Well, here goes nothing," he sighed, then locating the bell, he pushed it firmly.

"Mac! What are you doing? Are you mad? He's sure to have a gun, and there's probably an alarm system he could set off, and that will be the end of us."

"Maybe not," Mac said determinedly. "Let's see what happens." At that Mac pressed repeatedly on the bell, the sound echoing loudly through the silent halls. "Give me one of your shoes!"

"What?"

"Your high heel; take it off and give it to me—quick!" he demanded. Kim looked at him doubtfully, but quickly complied.

Just then they heard the lock click and the heavy metal door started moving slowly inward. Mac pulled Kim quickly behind him and stood to the side of the door, gripping the high-heeled slipper in his large fist. They stood breathless, as the door opened and Dr. Bronstein leaned out into the corridor.

"What is this? You know I am not to be disturbed when I am…"

He never got any further. The sharp heel with the force of 220 lbs of ex-soldier behind it came down hard on his head and he slumped forward into the hallway at their feet.

"Oh, Mac. He's alright? You didn't kill him, did you?" Kim cried.

Mac moved quickly. He felt the man's pulse and it was beating strongly; then he picked him up and pushed his way into the interior of the laboratory, Kim following him. "He's okay, but he'll be out for a while. See if you can find something I can tie him up with."

Kim pushed the door almost closed and turned around. Both she and Mac stood gazing at the very last thing they would have expected.

The room was a highly sophisticated scientific laboratory, equipped with bank after bank of computers and what they were sure was the latest, most expensive equipment available. The computer banks were flashing with lights, and varied sounds were being emitted from them. All in all, it was what it must have been like to walk into Dr. Frankenstein's laboratory for the first time. More like something out of Star Wars, Kim thought. It was like stepping into the future.

The strange, muted odor that had permeated the hallway was stronger in here, and she almost felt like coughing. Mac moved quickly, looking for rope or something with which to tie the doctor. "Wow!" Mac breathed. "Will you look at this place! What do you suppose...?"

Mac stopped dead in his tracks as he turned to look at Kim. She was white as a sheet, with a look of such profound fear that his heart leaped within him. He hadn't seen her like this since the first night he had found her in the alleyway when he had rescued her from certain death.

He grabbed her just in time as she collapsed into a dead faint. He held her close, felt the unreasonable coldness of her small body against him—comforting her, and as she slowly came back to consciousness, she gasped and started to cry.

"What is it, honey? What's the matter?"

"I don't know," she choked out. "I don't know, but something about this place terrifies me. There's something familiar about it. Oh, Mac, I hate it! Get me out of here, Mac. Right now! I have an awful feeling something horrible is going to happen!"

"Don't be silly, darling. It's just this weird room. Nothing's going to happen to you while I'm alive to prevent it."

"No, Mac. You don't understand. This is something terrible. We must go NOW!" She tried to pull out of his arms toward the door, but he held her closer to him.

"Honey, you know we can't. We have no place to run to. I just have to find that door. Now, calm down and help me tie up the doctor, then we'll find the door. We'll be out of here before morning and everything will be all right." Mac heard his own comforting words but for some reason, he didn't quite believe them himself. He only knew this place made his spine tingle, and all he wanted in the world at that moment was to get Kim and himself safely out of this house.

"I'm all right now, Mac. I'll help." She didn't sound very convincing, but she did pull herself up tall and start looking around the room for something to tie the doctor. In a corner, she found a laundry basket, and they took the dirty linen towels out and tore them into strong, narrow strips. With these, Mac tied the doctor securely. As an afterthought, he tore off a smaller strip and wadded it up, placing it in the doctor's mouth as a gag, in case he woke before they were finished.

"I'd sure like to know what they're up to in here. Looks like some pretty expensive equipment," Mac pondered.

"I don't know and I don't want to know," Kim shuddered. "Let's find that damned door."

"Let's just pray the door isn't behind these computer banks. If it is, we're sunk for sure." Mac stated, as he walked along the rows of flashing computers.

At the end of the row, they found a narrow metal door with a large latch arm. "Let's see what's in here," Mac suggested.

"No!" Kim's voice rang out, startling Mac in its intensity.

"Kim, honey. What is the matter? It's just a door."

"Don't open it, Mac. Please don't open it. I have a terrible feeling about what we might find. Please!" she pleaded.

"Come on now, honey. Calm down. I've never seen you act this way. Where's my big, brave girl?" She just stared at him with frightened, pleading eyes. "It's on the right side of the building. The door to the outside could very well be on the far wall of this room. We have to look!"

She clutched at his arm frantically. "No, Mac, please!!"

"Look, honey. You don't have to go in. I'll do it. You wait right out here. It won't take me a minute. Okay?"

She just stared at him, her large, almond-shaped eyes wide with fear.

Mac lifted the heavy arm with some effort and pushed open the metal door. A draft of very cold air hit him, and he realized this room was some kind of cold storage compartment. He pushed into the room and stopped.

Down both sides of the room were long, oblong tables covered with white sheets. Under the draped sheets he could make out what appeared to be human shapes.

Mac's stomach turned a few flip-flops, and his mouth felt dry. He tried to swallow, but there was nothing to swallow. "No wonder it smelled like a morgue," he thought. "What in the hell could they be doing with all these bodies? And where did they get them?"

He found himself moving toward the table nearest him. He felt revulsion turn in his guts, but something seemed to be pulling him toward it—some mysterious force that was more powerful than his own fears.

He steeled himself to take hold of the sheet and then, gulping in a lung-full of cold air, he quickly pulled it back.

What lay before him was a beautiful, young woman. Mac wondered at how lifelike she appeared even in death. Her color was good, and her skin looked firm—and—she was so young. Mac wondered what could have taken the life of so healthy-looking a girl.

Mac went from table to table now, his curiosity overcoming his sense of repulsion, and it was the same in every case; young, lovely healthy-looking girls.

As he pulled aside the sheet on the last table, he experienced a feeling of total disbelief at what he saw there. Then his heart nearly leaped out of his body when a piercing scream filled the small room.

He turned quickly to see Kim standing a few feet behind him, staring at the sight on the table in a complete state of shock. As he reached out his hand to her, she crumpled into a heap on the floor at his feet.

At this very moment, up in the library, Kato was lifting a large bottle of Seagram's 7 out of the liquor cabinet, when he noticed a dusty footprint on the carpet near the desk. He sat the bottle on the floor and traced the footprints to the fireplace. He scratched his head in bewilderment, then deciding there was something definitely wrong, he headed for the winding front stairs to check on the prisoners.

Mac's mind was still spinning, but before he could further investigate the phenomenon on the table, he had to take care of his Kim. He lifted her gently in his arms and headed toward the door. Then he remembered his purpose in coming into this room in the first place.

"Sorry, honey. I just have to see if that damned door is in here." He sat Kim gently down, her back resting against the wall near the inside door. He took off his jacket and wrapped it around her, concerned at her lack of response.

"I'll only be a moment." He stooped to kiss her forehead, and pulled back in surprise at how cold her skin already felt. She slumped against the wall. He knew he had to get her out of here soon, so he hurried to the outside wall. He searched every inch of the wall to no avail. All there was on that side was a lot of wall space and a barred window. He was about to give up, then took a look at the window again, and going on instinct, he took his nail clippers out of his back pocket and scratched where the window would continue down to the floor. He was elated to discover that the window was, indeed, the upper part of a door, which had been spackled closed and painted over.

He turned back toward Kim, his excitement showing on his face, only to see the large, metal door traveling the last few inches as it slammed tightly closed, trapping them inside the cold storage room. He rushed to the door, hoping to catch it before it closed entirely, thinking it had swung closed on its own. But it didn't budge. He heard the large latch handle as it closed down, locking them securely in the icy darkness.

The latch could not have fallen into place by itself. It was too heavy. It had to be pulled into position, and that took some amount of force.

Someone had locked them in. Someone who knew they were there and wanted them dead.

He rubbed his arms with his hands, feeling the icy coldness creep into his bones. Only part of the cold came from the room, the rest came from the fear that took hold of his guts and squeezed them dry. He stood there, helpless in his shirtsleeves, knowing how stupid he had been not to think of something like this happening.

He looked down at Kim, his eyes now adjusted to the darkness and made out enough of her form to see she was still out.

He sank down beside her and reached out for her. What would happen to them now? Would they end their lives together in this morgue-like room?

He pulled Kim into his arms and wrapped his arms and legs around her, trying in vain to warm up her cold, limp body.

As he sat there, holding her close to him, his mind raced with conjectures. Who had locked them in this refrigerator? He doubted it could have been the doctor, as he had been tied too securely. Had Kato come back? Were they going to leave them in there to die? Oh, what had he done to this sweet, trusting girl in his arms? She had faith in him, and he had led her into this trap.

Well, it didn't do any good to speculate on it. If whoever locked them in didn't let them out before morning, they'd be dead anyway. He thought about working at the door to see if he could get it open, but he knew it would probably be a waste of time, and in the meantime, Kim would freeze to death. No he had to stay with her.

He adjusted Kim's body so that they lay so entwined together that the air could only hit them on two sides. Then he tucked the jacket as closely about them as possible. He cradled her head on his arm and buried his face in her soft, silky hair.

He would have to stay awake! It was the only way to keep her from freezing. He must not go to sleep!

He awoke a few moments later to the sound of tapping. He was so cold he couldn't get his brain to function properly for a minute or two. Then, it finally dawned on him that the tapping sounds were coming from the outer wall of the building.

Stoner! It had to be Stoner. His heart leaped into his throat. It wasn't too late after all!

He tried to move, but found that his body was stiff with cold. The tapping sound came again. He managed to get his left arm free and peered at the luminous letters on his watch. It was 4:15. Stoner had said he would only stay at the door until a little after 3:00 AM. He was taking a big chance in waiting this long.

Mac had to get to that door!

He used all the energy he had to force his legs to move. He was torn between the need to get to the walled-up door and somehow get it open, and staying close to Kim so she wouldn't freeze.

Finally, he decided to see if he could drag them both over to the window. It was about 15 feet, a long, long way.

He moved slowly, pulling himself a few inches at a time, his cold muscles aching with the strain—pulling Kim along with him.

Fifteen minutes later, they reached the outer wall and he reached up and tapped on the door. He tapped again as hard as his frozen muscles would allow, and he laid back waiting and praying for the answer taps that would tell him Stoner was still there and now knew where the hidden door was.

He had a hard time staying awake, listening, and fighting the unconsciousness that wanted to claim him.

He dozed. Then he heard it. He knew he had heard it! Yes, it was a sharp tapping noise outside the window door. Stoner had found them. Now they would be safe!

He was reaching up to tap again on the door, when the other sound came to him, chilling him more than the cold of the room.

It was a loud, metallic sound that grated on his spine. Then the heavy inner door swung open and light flooded into the room.

Mac's arms tightened around Kim protectively. So close. They had been so close!

As his eyes became accustomed to the bright light, he made out the evil leering face of Kato bending over them.

He looked down into Kim's white face. She was still breathing, thank God, but he knew she wouldn't last much longer.

Kato kicked him hard in the ribs, and he could feel the coldly brittle bones crack.

"Come on, get up! The boss wants to talk to you!" hissed Kato.

CHAPTER

Fifteen

Mac moved slowly, getting his frozen muscles working as he struggled to his feet. He lifted Kim gently and headed slowly toward the door, stumbling from time to time under the weight of the unconscious girl. He could feel the blessed warm air envelop them as he staggered into the laboratory. He was so glad to be alive and out of cold storage that even Kai looked good to him.

Kai was standing in the middle of the room, his most charming smile on his lips. One could almost have believed he was glad to see them, so warm was his welcome.

Kai had Kato wrap a large warm wool blanket around Mac and Kim, whose head rested lightly on Mac's shoulder. Mac looked down at her small, innocent face—so lovely whether in repose or full of mischief—or expressing the passion and love she felt for him. He had sure let her down. Whatever Kai had in store for them, it probably wouldn't be much better than the fate they had faced in the cold storage room.

Kato was none too gentle in his unwilling ministrations. He glared at Kai. "What's the point of this? You promised them to me, and I was having fun watching them freeze through the window slot. My only regret was that they were able to be together. I'm sorry I called you at all," he hissed.

Kai smiled at his impatient friend. "Patience, my friend. It won't be long now. I just have a few points to clear up with my friend, Mac, then you can have them both, with my blessings."

~

Stoner waited until 4:45, hidden in the bushes near the outside of the laboratory wall. It had stopped raining, but it was freezing cold and an icy wind tore at his wet gardener's jacket and up the legs of his work pants.

He thought at one point that he had heard tapping from within the basement, but he hadn't heard it again. He looked at his watch for the 200th time since 2:00 AM.

He knew he had to go. It was foolhardy to stay here as long as he had. He didn't even know for sure if Neely and the girl had been able to get to the basement through the secret passage. And if, when they got to the basement, they were able to get to the outside wall. There were just too damned many "ifs" to this whole thing. He wondered, too, if they had been able to find the safe. Oh, hell. He'd try to get back up to that window somehow tomorrow night and see if he could find out what was happening.

He stifled a yawn, then moved as quietly as possible to look out through the thick bushes. He could hardly get his legs to work, he had been crouching there in the cold for so long.

"Might as well call it a night," he thought. He crept stealthily from behind the bushes, and made his way silently along the side of the house, pressing his body as close to the bushes as possible. He'd go back to the gardener's cottage and take a hot shower. Tomorrow was another day, and all he could think about now was that warm water washing away the dirt and the chill. "Boy, that bed will sure feel good tonight," he sighed.

He was just clearing the corner of the mansion and starting silently to cross the garden to his cottage, when he felt a sharp pain on the top of his skull and darkness descended upon him—a painful darkness which forced him down, down, down, into an oblivion he would never leave.

Mac sat dejectedly cradling Kim in his arms, the blanket having warmed them, but his side ached dreadfully, and when he tried to take a deep breath, he was wracked with sharp, piercing pains. He knew he must have a couple of broken ribs.

Kim had still not regained consciousness, but her breathing was even, and she was once again warm in his arms. He decided she was in no immediate danger.

He looked up at Kai who was pacing the floor in front of him. The scientist was nowhere in sight. Kato leaned against one of the computer banks, toying ominously with his knife.

"You really are a very naughty boy, you know, Mac. Dr. Bronstein, my best scientist, is suffering from a slight concussion. We had to send for an ambulance, but you'll be happy to hear he has been patched up and sent home for the night," Kai smiled.

"Hooray," Mac offered, cheerlessly.

"Oh, you may not be too impressed, but he is really very valuable to us. More valuable than you could ever imagine. Without him, our trillion-dollar industry would have been quite impossible. He's really a genius, you know, in his field."

"His field? And what might that be, if I may be so bold?" Mac jibbed, then getting angry again, he added, "Just what the hell are you slobs up to, anyway? And what's with all that in the cold storage?"

Just then they were interrupted by one of the guards, who came to the laboratory door. Kato went over and spoke a few words to him; the guard nodded and took off. Kato resumed his place near the computer, polishing his knife on his trouser leg, and watching Mac like a cat ready to pounce.

"You were about to tell me about the bodies in the cold storage," Mac prompted.

"Oh yes, that's right. You still don't know about our girls, do you, Mr. Neely? Well, I don't suppose there's any harm in telling you now. You'll not be leaving here alive anyway."

"It won't work, Kai. The police know where we are."

"Oh," smiled Kai. "You mean your friend, the gardener?"

Mac's heart sank.

"My, yes. He was a clever one. Nearly had us all fooled. Unfortunately for him, Kato was watching you through the slit window, enjoying your suffering. He thought it was odd that you worked so hard to get over to tap on the wall under that window.

"That guard you just saw was sent out to investigate. I'm afraid your policeman friend won't be making any more reports. So, you see, you're quite at our mercy."

"Mercy! Huh, you don't even know what the word means," Mac rasped.

"Now how can you say that, Neely?" Kai purred. "Look at how nice we're treating you and your 'lady'. We truly want you to enjoy your last few minutes of life. Now, surely that is merciful." He broke out in a peak of his evil laughter, and even Kato allowed himself to look pleased. After all, didn't he have a lot to look forward to? He could almost feel the knife in his hand slipping through this cocky bastard's flesh.

Mac sighed and adjusted Kim so that the weight was on his other side, away from the cracked and painful ribs. "You were going to tell me what you're up to. You can start with the girls in the storage room."

"Oh, yes, the girls. The girls are my fortune. The heart of my whole industry." He turned to Kato. "Kato, will you kindly bring one of my young ladies out."

"That's hardly necessary. I saw the bodies when I was in there," Mac stated wearily.

"Oh, but you didn't see what makes them so special—so valuable!" Kai said with enthusiasm. "I'm really very proud of them. They are almost ready to be put to work for me."

Mac's brain was spinning. He was hearing the words, but in his mind, he was seeing the bodies on the tables sheathed in their white sheets—then that last table—yes, that was different. What was it? His brain was so tired. All he wanted to do was sleep—sleep away the pain—sleep away the fear—the hopelessness.

Yes, it was coming back to him now—what he had seen on that table—what it was that had made Kim scream and fall into this comatose state. He remembered, but the implications were too awful. He didn't want to remember.

As Kato re-entered the laboratory from the cold storage vault, he carried in his arms one of the girls Mac had hidden earlier. Kai's voice came to him through his confusion.

"I'm really very proud of them, you know. They are even more sophisticated than their predecessors, who are already bringing me in thousands of dollars a day."

"Predecessors?" Mac frowned. "I don't understand."

"Do you want me to activate her, Boss?" Kato urged.

"No, Kato. She would have to be thoroughly thawed out first and that would take too much time, I'm afraid. Just place her here on the floor and open the flap." Kato complied as Mac watched in fascination. "Mr. Neely should be very interested in this. After all, he has a stake in our project now."

Mac glared at him, trying to get his brain functioning; trying to figure out what the man was saying. His ears heard, but his brain was rejecting it. When he looked back at the lovely young girl sitting on the floor opposite them, he was staring into an exposed section of her chest. It was boxlike and contained a myriad of wires and connections which looked strangely like computer components.

He stared at it in disbelief. This was what he had seen on that last table and his brain had refused to accept. He was grateful that Kim was still unconscious and not forced to see this. He could hear Kai chuckle as he stared at the monstrous thing before him.

"Yes, you've heard of them, haven't you, Neely? Some call them androids, but we prefer to call them humanoids. You must admit, they are certainly worthy of that name." He laughed. "And you of all people, should attest to that."

"But, how...why??" Mac sputtered.

"Why? It should be quite obvious by now, Mr. Neely. They make excellent prostitutes. Docile in nature, but as you have already discovered, very passionate in nature." Kai smirked.

"Are you trying to tell me you manufacture these...things...to use in whorehouses?" Mac gasped.

"Oh, my heavens, no. That would be a sinful waste. These girls are top of the line. They are sold for top dollar to international cartels to please their most elite clients. They're really worth it. They possess all the advantages of a woman and none of the disadvantages. For instance, they never grow old, never lose their youthful zest, and truly enjoy their work. Thank goodness these later models are more compliant than our Kim." He watched Mac's face closely.

Mac looked away from the android and turned to face Kai. He searched Kai's leering face for some indication that what he was implying was not true, but he saw there only the face of the cat that had his mouse where he wanted him and was enjoying to the full playing that last ace.

"What are you trying to tell me?" Mac whispered, fear bubbling up into his throat and choking him.

"It's difficult for me to believe you haven't figured it out on your own by now. Are you really so blind, or won't your Irish pride let you admit that you've made a complete fool of yourself?" Kai was thoroughly enjoying Mac's discomfort. "Is she really that well-made?"

Mac would have leaped out of the chair and grabbed Kai by the throat except for the girl in his arms. "You smiling son-of-a-bitch! Are you implying that my Kim is one of these...these?"

"Humanoids, Mr. Neely. You don't mind if I don't call you Mac, You see, I don't like you very much."

Mac started to rise, but Kato was immediately at his side, so he sank back into the chair, afraid to look at Kim—afraid of what he was feeling.

"She is a very special humanoid, though, Mr. Neely. My first—the original model, and therefore very dear to my heart—until she took it into her head to run away. We haven't figured how that could have happened yet."

"Dr. Bronstein designed her, and it was his genius that produced her. Her defection is still a mystery to us, but Bronstein is trying to circumvent it ever happening again in the newer models. She somehow turned out too human. So human, it even scares me at times."

Mac stared at him, his tired mind refusing to accept the terrifying knowledge that Kai was revealing to him.

"In fact, it was these too-human qualities in Kim that made us decide to destroy her. She seemed somehow to have developed a will of her own. She had emotions she wasn't supposed to have, and we found we had little control over those emotions. She actually refused to become a prostitute and ran away! Can you believe it? Ran away from me—her creator. Unheard of!"

"Then you came along and rescued her, and she developed this unholy attachment to you. Strange, to say the least."

Mac could contain himself no longer. He jumped up, cradling Kim in his arms, heading blindly toward Kai in a rage of hurt and anger. "You dirty, lying son of a bitch! Damn your rotten piss-filled mind!"

Kato was upon him before he moved two steps and he felt the cold steel of the knife pry into his wounded ribs. He cried out in pain and stopped.

He felt Kim move in his arms and looked down at her. Her eyes were wide open and she was staring at the ceiling.

"Kim! Kim!" he cried, fear in the very marrow of his bones. She didn't seem to hear him, but once again went limp in his arms, dropping into blessed oblivion again. He was not sure if she had been conscious enough to hear Kai's revelation, but prayed with all his heart that she hadn't been. From somewhere in the distance, he heard Kai's evil laughter. His mind swirled. It must be a lie! Kai was just telling him this horrible thing to hurt him, to make him suffer. It couldn't be true, not his Kim! It was impossible!!!

"I can prove it to you, if you like," Kai sneered. "Just a little cut..." He took a step toward the pair.

Mac pulled Kim close in his arms and glared at Kai. "If you so much as lay a filthy finger on her, I'll kill you!" It was said in such deadly earnest that Kai was forced to take a step backward.

"A brave threat for one in your present position, my friend. You are a fool, Neely! Willing to fight and risk your life over a piece of machinery...a gadget...a figment of my imagination...a junky piece of circuitry and components."

Before Mac knew what he was doing, he had let Kim slip to the floor and was at Kai's throat. Anger and frustration welled up in him so strongly that he could taste the bile in his throat—anger against this beast whose vile flesh he was squeezing in a vise-like grip—angry that what Kai said might be the truth—angry at his own sense of hopeless frustration and shock!

Kai was too surprised at first to defend himself, but now he was fighting back, his own frustrations finding a welcome outlet in Mac's muscular body. His face was distorted with rage and the lack of oxygen, while his delicate but strong hands fought to loosen Mac's grip on his throat.

Kato moved quickly toward the two struggling opponents, intent on ending the fight with a well-aimed knife in Mac's back, but Kai, having loosened Mac's hold on his throat, rasped out instructions for Kato to stay out of it. Kai was fighting back now, exulting in the pure physical release, his own anger at the boiling point, being fed by his hatred and jealousy of this guttersnipe of a bartender, who could inspire love even from a machine. Kai had *never inspired love in anyone*—even his own mother had hated him for his cold, cruel nature. In his anger, he was unaware that he was as *guilty of attachment to his mechanical creation* as Mac was. It was a matter of ownership—possession. **Kim was his!** If she was going to defy all logic and love with a human's depth of emotion—*she had to love him,* Kai. Nobody else!! He had lived his whole life on the edge of madness, and now in this moment of possessive jealousy, he toppled gladly over the brink.

Even as the truth formed in his distorted mind, he had to laugh at himself. *"Jealous over a humanoid! It was just too funny!"* The room was filled with his evil laughter.

Kai's laughter made Mac's anger and frustration turn to rage, and he maneuvered Kai in front of him with a sudden burst of energy and got him in a stranglehold that would surely break his neck. Kai struggled, but knew he was in deep trouble. He managed to rasp out, "Kato!"

Kato, finally freed of all restrictions, was exultant. At last, he was going to have his chance at this man—this bartender—who had become the object of his most intense hatred. If you had asked him why he hated Mac so deeply, he could not have given a reason. It was an emotion without and beyond reason. He had just sensed disaster when he had first seen Mac, and the feeling persisted still. To kill Mac would be to kill the nagging fear within him.

A smirking grin spread across Kato's face as he raised his knife in the air above Mac's defenseless back. Mac closed his eyes and gave Kai's neck a strong jerking squeeze. He felt Kai go limp in his arms.

Kato stood still at Mac's back. His arm with the sharp ugly knife still poised, an expression of total bewilderment on his face. He watched his knife slip out of his hand and clatter noisily to the floor. He couldn't seem to move. He was vaguely conscious of an uncomfortable feeling in the middle of his back, but it was hard to pin it down as the room, for some strange reason was getting dark... darker...darker....

Kim stared at the portion of broken glass test tube that stuck out of Kato's back, watching in fascination as the blood spread across his jacket and he slumped forward and fell with a crash to the floor at her feet.

Mac didn't see any of this. He was just loosening his hold on Kai's neck, thinking he was unconscious.

Kai twisted suddenly, his ruse having worked, and taking Mac off guard, he managed to get his hand on the gun that was in his back pocket. Mac, struggling to retain his loosened stranglehold, felt his muscles tiring. His side shot arrows of pain over the whole side of his body. His mind leaped back into the battle as he heard the click of the safety as Kai readied his pistol to fire. Mac let go of Kai's throat and grabbed at his wrist.

Mac was aware that even in as good a physical condition as he was, he couldn't keep this up much longer. But somehow, he had to. This

A BARTENDER'S HOLIDAY | 125

was a life-and-death struggle. He gritted his teeth and called forth a last burst of energy.

They struggled over the gun. Kai had managed to point the gun at Mac's mid-section, and was fighting to pull the trigger, but Mac was squeezing the artery at Kai's wrist and pushing with all his might to shove the gun aside. Mac took a deep breath, feeling the pains shoot against his injured ribs, and pushed. Suddenly Kai's grip relaxed for a second due to the lack of blood supply into his hand. It was all Mac needed to push the gun a few inches away from his body. As the gun exploded, Mac felt a searing pain on his rib case under his arm.

Kai pulled the trigger again and Mac heard a piercing scream as the stray bullet hit a computer bank and sparks started flying at them.

The computer hissed and sputtered, and finally exploded, knocking Kim, Mac, and Kai against the far wall.

Flames shot out from the computer bank, now in shambles as the fire and explosions increased until the whole side of the room was in flames.

Mac pulled himself up, shaking his head to clear it, and looked around him. Kai was unconscious. Mac couldn't tell if he was dead or not, and he wasn't going to take the time to find out. Kim! He had to find Kim!

He found her lying next to Kato's bloody body. His heart nearly stopped. Was she dead? Oh, Lord, let her not be dead! He bent down and felt her pulse. She was still alive. Thank God. He lifted her gently, but quickly, the heat from the flames burning his skin and searing his throat and lungs.

He searched her face, seeing her eyes open. She looked up at him and the tears started flowing down her soot-covered cheeks. She smiled and his heart flip-flopped.

"Oh, my love," he crooned. "You're alive! Come, sweetheart, we're going to get out of here."

The heat was getting unbearable. He struggled toward the door with Kim in his arms, tripping over debris from the explosions. He breathed a prayer of thanks that the heavy metal door to the hallway had been left ajar. Kim held on to him hard, her arms entwined about his neck, as he used his right foot to kick the debris out of the path of the door and put his hand through the slit in the door, using what strength he had left to pull the heavy door open. He winced as the metal door burnt his hand, but a few seconds later they were both safely out in the hallway.

Kim was trembling uncontrollably. "Mac, let me down now. I can walk. We can go faster if I walk."

He hesitated, but decided she was right. He gently set her down, but as her feet hit the floor, she collapsed against him. "Maybe I'd better carry you, honey," he offered, but she pulled herself together with all her strength, and pulled away from him, standing a little wobbly but surely on her own feet.

She smiled a brave little smile. "Which way, Mac?"

He paused for a moment to get his bearings. They had two choices. They could go up the stairs to the house, but the possibility of running into some of the armed guards made that pretty tricky.

Their only alternative seemed to be the way they had come down. Only that would take more time than he would have liked to take, as the flames were now shooting out the door of the lab and the heat in the hallway was becoming unbearable.

"What about the way we came?" Kim offered.

He smiled at her, hiding his fears behind a brave front. "Elementary, my dear Ms. Watson." He grabbed her hand, and they ran toward the alcove where the heavy files barred their way to safety.

They started to work trying to move the heavy file cabinets, but both of them were weak and tired, and it seemed like an impossible task. It was getting hotter by the minute and the hall was fast filling up with smoke.

Suddenly Mac stopped and slapped his forehead in frustration. "Stupid! Where the hell's my head? We're on this side now."

Kim looked at him in bewilderment.

"The drawers!" he cried. She caught his meaning immediately, and they worked together to remove the heavy drawers, packed full of old musty files.

He pulled on the files, minus the drawers, but the files still proved obstinate. "They're stuck behind that ridge in the cement. That's why we had so much trouble pushing them out before. If only I could get behind them and push, but it's just too damned narrow."

"I can fit, I think," Kim coughed. "No, no, I'm okay now, Mac. I want to do it." Mac pulled out his hankie and handed it to Kim, who tied it around her face. She squeezed in between the wall and the filing cabinet and pushed against it with all of her might.

Mac pulled at the same time, and finally, with a great creaking noise, the cabinet cleared the obstacle of roughened cement, and moved away from the doorway enough for Mac to push in beside Kim. The combined effort worked, and a moment later the doorway was cleared enough for Mac to insert his fingers through the opening and pull the door open enough for them to squeeze through.

He pushed Kim through first, and pushed in after her, pulling the panel closed behind them. The air was musty, but at least the smoke had not yet penetrated to any great extent. They both took in a big gulp of air.

Mac put his arm around Kim and they ascended the stairs quickly.

When they reached the main floor, Mac felt around for the latch to let them out into the library. They squeezed through the trap door and stepped out into the library. From here on, if they could avoid the guards, they would be home free.

Mac felt better than he had in days. In a short while this whole nightmare would be over. He and Kim would be able to live like normal human beings.

Kai's jeering words about Kim came back to him, but he brushed them aside. It wasn't true, and even if it was…

At that moment, there was a tremendously loud explosion that shook the house from top to bottom. Wood flew from the paneling, a large, ragged hole appeared in the center of the library floor, allowing smoke and flames to shoot upward into the room.

Mac yelled as Kim's hand was torn from his grasp and she was thrown backward. He struggled to free himself from the fireplace, where he had been thrown, just as a huge ceiling beam fell from the rafters above them, pinning both of them to the floor. The sound of

Kim's scream echoed in his ears, his heart pounded, the heat was scorching his skin, his eyes burned, and the smoke was choking him. The pain in his lungs was almost unbearable.

He pulled himself up and was just able to extricate his leg from a mass of lumber and plaster, but there was a long gash in his calf which was bleeding profusely. Other than that, he seemed to be in one piece.

Kim?? Where was Kim? He couldn't see her through all the smoke. His heart pounded in fear, the pain of anxiety worse than the pain in his leg and ribs.

The flames were spreading now, eating up the priceless, torn oriental carpet, reaching up to engulf the rich velvet and satin drapery.

He HAD to get to Kim! Oh, God, he had to get her out of there before the whole house was engulfed in flames. He just HAD to! He knew now, beyond the shadow of a doubt, that he loved her, no matter who or what she was. He loved her! She was his life, his Joy!

He thought of the tear in her side, and leaned down and kissed her lips tenderly. "My silly, silly, pumpkin. How could you even consider such a thing? You know Kai was a psychopathic liar. He'd have done or said anything to destroy our love. A love he could never understand, or never hope to inspire. He was insanely jealous—and a madman!"

She looked up at him pleadingly. "Then it's not true? I am a woman? I want to be a woman for you, Mac. I love you so much, my darling. So very, very much. No one could love so much if they didn't have a heart, could they, Mac? Could they?"

"Of course not, my love. Don't even think about it. Save your strength. We have to get you out of here, fast." He choked and coughed, finding it harder and harder to breathe. He leaned closer and pressed his lips on hers again.

"Oh, yes, darling. Kiss me, kiss me a million times. I'll never get enough of your kisses." He could feel her struggling to respond and then, agonizingly, he felt her go limp. He pulled back and looked at her, and knew in his heart that she had left him. The flames were getting dangerously close to the young couple, but Mac didn't feel them any longer. He laid his cheek against hers and cried like a baby, not caring to live anymore without her.

CHAPTER

Sixteen

Why was he hurting? His whole body ached. He felt heat, lots of heat. Who was pulling at him?

He was in the midst of a great fog. No. Smoke. It was smoke. Someone was tugging at his arm, pulling at him.

He reacted with anger, pushing away the bothersome hands.

"Mac! Mr. Neely! You must come! We've got to get out of here!" Mac heard the husky male voice as if at the end of a long tunnel.

"Mac!" Lindham cried. "For God's sake man, come on! There's nothing you can do for her now. Nothing anyone can do." He knew he couldn't and wouldn't move, would never leave her here alone.

All of a sudden, he felt a sharp pain as something hard landed on his jaw. He mercifully sank into unconsciousness again.

It was a long way up, much longer this time. Why was it so far? He felt cold and he didn't like it. He wanted to stay in his nice cozy, black cocoon. It would be so easy just to float away and never have to think again, never have to feel...

However, something—perhaps his deepest self—decided otherwise, and he found himself struggling upward out of the darkness into the harshness of reality.

Why was everything red, he wondered. Maybe he was dead... maybe this was hell.

He blinked his eyes. Yes. It must be hell—all this pain, cold and pain now—not heat and pain, but just as bad. It was a living hell, and the flames of the mansion leaped and crackled in the center of it.

But he wasn't in it. He tried to sit up. He could see the mansion now in front of him, about 100 feet away. It was consumed in flames a beautiful and horrifying sight.

He fell back. Why couldn't he sit up properly?

And then he remembered Kim. She was in that flaming volcano. He pulled himself up with great effort and pain, realizing at last that he was tied to a stretcher. He pushed at the ties with his arms, but they were tightly secured.

He let out a scream of rage and frustration, and started fighting against his bonds. He had to go to Kim. He couldn't go back to a life without her. It would be meaningless.

"You're not going anywhere, Mac." It was Lt. Lindham's voice. Lindham sat down beside the stretcher and put his hand gently on Mac's shoulder. "Don't fight it, man. It won't do any good."

He wanted to cry out at the injustice of it, to turn his upside-down world right-side-up by pure needing, but he knew it wouldn't work. He slumped back onto the stretcher, hopelessness possessing him, his heart feeling tight and restricted in his chest.

"I'm going through my own hell, Mac," Lindham sighed. "If we had only been a little sooner, things might have been different."

Then it struck Mac. "But, how did you know where to find us? Kai said they killed Stoner."

"We never have just one plant on a job like this. Stoner didn't know we had another man working with him. Thought he'd be safer if he didn't know. Our other man saw them finish Stoner in the garden. He wasn't close enough to save him, but he got out of here fast and phoned us. We got here just in time to hear the initial explosion in the basement. It was pure blind luck that I found you in the library."

Mac looked at the concerned man beside him. "I haven't thanked you, Lindham. You saved my life. Though at the moment, I'm not too sure that was a blessing."

"Think nothing of it. It's one of the more satisfying aspects to our business. But the ambulance men are waiting for you. I said I needed a couple of minutes with you. I know you're in pain, but if you could answer just a couple of questions, it would help us get started on this mess."

"Go ahead. I'm okay," Mac lied.

"Did you find out what they were up to down there in that basement?" Lindham urged.

Mac explained as briefly as he could about the laboratory and the "humanoid" prostitute ring, but left out the fact that Kim had had any part in it. He was exhausted and angry again when he finished. "I can only thank God that that monster Kai Ching is dead, too."

Just then the ambulance drivers came toward them from the rear of the mansion. Two policemen were following them, carrying a stretcher.

As they neared Mac and Lindham, Mac saw, in the red glare of the flames, the face of a man he never wanted to see again, a face framed in ash-streaked blond hair. The face was burned badly, but grotesque though it was, there was no mistaking Mac's nemesis, Kai Ching.

"Looks like you spoke too soon, Mac," offered Lindham.

As the stretcher drew adjacent to Mac and Lindham, Mac grabbed Lindham's arm. Lindham motioned to the ambulance attendants, and they brought the stretcher over near Mac and set it down gently on the ground beside him.

Mac pulled himself painfully to a sitting position and stared down at the smoke-blackened form on the stretcher beside him. The grotesque red mask that had taken the place of Kai's handsome face sickened Mac, but he recognized the evil gleam in the eyes that were nearly swollen closed. He knew the man must be in terrible pain, but his hateful spirit lent him a strength that frightened Mac even now. A hideous laugh rang out on the cold night air, clouded now by smoke from the quickly diminishing flames of the mansion.

"So, you survived after all," Kai laughed, then added sarcastically. "The fate of the 'truly good', I hear." Mac cringed. "But I hear you lost your little 'doll'. Too bad, sucker!" His laugh rang out again.

It was all Mac could do not to break his bonds and sink his fist into the pulpy red mass of Kai's face. Hatred spread through him like the flames that spread through the mansion. Only Lindham's restraining hand on his shoulder, providing a bit of reality in this nightmare, kept him from strangling the monster on the stretcher beside him. "You filthy…" Mac couldn't even speak he was so incensed.

Kai laughed again. "You thought I was dead, huh? Sorry to disappoint you. I was only dazed. I got out of the room right after you but you had disappeared, so I went up the stairs leading into the house. I was trying to get into my safe when the room exploded. The next thing I knew these kind gentlemen were putting me on a stretcher, and here I am. You can't keep a good man down, huh Mac?" This seemed to amuse him even more, and his triumphant laughter rang out again, lifting the hackles on everyone's back. Lindham waited for the laughter to die down, then looked down at Kai.

"That's right, Ching. Get a good laugh now. Get it all out of your system, because you won't find much to laugh at in prison!"

"Prison?" hissed Kai. "You fool. You'll never put Kai Ching in any prison. You can't hold me. You have no evidence. Mr. Neeley took care of that when he caused that bullet to blow up the computer banks."

"You're very much mistaken in that assumption, Ching," Lindham said. "We have all the evidence we need to send you up for the rest of your life!"

"Who do you think you're kidding?" Kai sneered. "The last of your evidence is drifting away with that smoke over there. I'll be out of the hospital in a few weeks, and free as a bird. And what I built once, I can build again!"

"I'm afraid you're wrong there, Kai," Lindham interposed. "We have all the evidence we'll need to convict you of international drug trafficking. By the time you get done serving time for that, you'll be too old to be worrying about prostitution."

Kai watched Lindham's face as he spoke, and feeling the sincerity of the agent, he felt the beginnings of fear rising in his throat. "That's impossible! You're bluffing. All my records, all evidence of what we were doing is in what's left of that house. My whole empire—all I created."

Mac watched Kai's eyes as Lindham spoke. "Sorry, Ching. I'm not bluffing. But I admit it would have been worth a try just to watch you squirm. No, Ching, you have as they say, been hoisted upon your own petard." Mac smiled inwardly at the thought this picture made.

"You see, Ching. It was one of your own creations which has finished you off."

"My creations?"

"Yes. The girl you educated and then used to your own advantage."

Mac and Kai spoke at the same time. "Kim?"

"Yes," Lindham affirmed. He looked at Mac. "We found the purse."

If a light went off inside of Kai, it went on in Mac's head.

The purse. That meant the dossier.

"It was at the police department storage room all the time," Lindham explained. "It was picked up by the patrolmen who reached the scene just after you had carried Kim out of the alley. When it was taken to the police storage, it got filed wrong, and thanks to an alert policewoman in the division, who dug it out, we now have the microfilm."

Mac felt like crying. Nothing could bring Kim back to him now, but at least she hadn't died in vain. She had wanted to destroy the evil that was Kai Ching—and now she had.

Lindham turned back to Kai Ching. "She also had a sample of your 'Happy Dust' which is in our labs now. It is only a matter of time till we get all the pieces put together, but I can assure you, it will be very neatly packaged by the time you go to court."

Kai's fear showed in his voice as he cried out, "You know it will never hold up in court without Kim as a witness. And you can't do a damn thing about that! You have to have a witness; and you don't have one!"

"Wrong again, Ching. We do have a witness. A very important one."

"You're bluffing!" Kai shouted, wincing in pain.

The ambulance attendant put a restraining hand on Kai's shoulder. "Take it easy, Mr." He turned to Lindham. "I don't mean to interfere sir, but both these men should be in the hospital."

Lindman nodded. "You're right. We're almost finished."

Kai Ching shouted and pulled away from the restraining hands of the attendant, trying to rise, but in too much pain. "What witness, God damn you! What witness?" he yelled.

"Quite a substantial one, Ching. A witness whose very occupation will lend credibility to his testimony. A man whose conscience finally got the best of him." Kai was straining to sit up now. The burnt flesh of his face beaded with perspiration in spite of the fevered skin. Mac watched Lindharm's face in suspense.

"We got a call from Mercy Hospital about a man with a skull fracture who was treated and released. They were suspicious because of what seemed like a confession of sorts that this man made when he was semi-conscious. They gave us his home address and we picked him up two hours ago. He told us what was going on at the mansion and is more than willing to testify if it will get him a lighter sentence. Claims he is a man of science and didn't know until recently what you were using your lovely ladies for." He smiled at Kai, who had sunk back lifelessly on the stretcher. "I think you'll find he will be witness enough." Lindham turned and smiled at Mac, who managed a small grin in return.

Mac watched the disintegration of Kai Ching before his very eyes. It was almost like someone had let the air out of a balloon. Nothing could ever make up for what Kai had done to Kim, for her final destruction, but he was destroyed now. He would never do any harm to anyone again with his mad schemes. Mac couldn't feel any pity for the creature before him, but it did seem that at that moment, some of the hatred and bitterness left his soul. He felt empty—a whole lot lost.

But he was alive, and the evil that was Kai Ching was destroyed. It had to mean something.

Mac and Lindham watched as the stretcher bearers lifted the lifeless form and headed toward the ambulance.

As the ambulance attendants returned and lifted Mac's stretcher, he took one last look at the blackened remains of the mansion, and the end of his hopes for happiness with Kim, he felt a tear trickle down his cheek. His lips formed silent words. "Goodbye my love. I'll never forget you."

Epilogue

Harlacher's voice droned on, as Mac straightened up the bar. Mac had been back to work for a week now. His ribs had healed pretty well, but he still limped slightly from the injury his leg had sustained from the falling beam. The burns on his hands and body still gave him occasional twinges of pain, but all in all, the two weeks stay in the hospital had put him back together pretty well, physically.

He hadn't told anyone what had happened while he was away. He just couldn't talk about it yet. Anyway, it was such a fantastic story, who would believe him. Besides, whoever listened to a bartender?

Joyce called out an order to him, and he automatically mixed the drinks. Paul sat at a back corner table going over the books. He had sure been lucky to find Paul. He had taken over the bar and run it with a sure touch while Mac was gone.

From time to time, he would catch Joyce or Paul looking at him with questions in their eyes, but mercifully, they never pressed him. They seemed to know he would tell them the whole story when he was ready. He had never realized that he had some good friends until now. He knew, he felt it, that these two people were genuinely concerned for him. It seemed to lighten his grief a little.

Well, he sighed, he had wanted to LIVE! And, he had been granted his wish. He guessed he had lived and loved and lost more and faster than most men. He had truly lived his whole life, the most important and meaningful part of it, at least, in those precious few days with Kim.

He could see her now. He always would. Her small oval face, the pale, glowing skin, the silken hair falling straight and soft to her waist. He saw her smile, could almost feel her small, warm body pressing against his.

But this type of thinking was not doing him any good. He had to stop thinking about her...stop remembering...stop living in the past...but HOW?

"She's already started divorce proceedings, Mac. My lawyer says she could take me for everything I've got! What should I do, Mac?" Harlacher looked on the verge of tears. "If you had only been here, this would never have happened. Where in hell were you, Mac? Where?" Harlacher wailed.

Mac looked at Harlacher, finally bringing his face into full focus. "Look, Harlacher, I'm not your psychiatrist or your mother. Here. Take this bottle. Go home and sleep it off. You got a good lawyer, the best in town. You'll do okay."

Harlacher got to his feet rather uncertainly, looked at the Fifth of Seagram's being held out to him, and not being able to resist, grabbed it and hugged it to his heart. "You're right, Mac. You're always right. No hard feelin's, huh? Just a little under the weather, ya know." With that he gave what he thought was one of his best smiles, turned, and clutching the bottle tightly, staggered out onto the street.

Mac watched him till the door swung closed behind him, then walked to the end of the bar and picked up a glass from the stack he had just sterilized. He polished it without thought, staring into the crystal image of his face in the side of the glass as he held it cradled in his palm.

He didn't even hear the soft voice the first time. "Mr. Neely?" She spoke louder. "Mr. Neely? You are Mr. Neely, aren't you? The waitress told me...."

He looked up into a heart-shaped face, with large black braids atop a proud young head.

His heart stopped. "Kim!"

"I'm sorry. I didn't mean to startle you." She looked at him with anxious, questioning eyes—almond-shaped brown eyes. "My name is Lian Ching."

Why was she giving him a phony name? "Lian Ching?" he questioned.

"Yes. Kai Ching was my brother."

"Brother?" Mac stared at her in shock. Lian Ching—Kai's sister? Not Kim? Of course, not Kim. Kim was dead, wasn't she? Mac was in a state of shocked confusion. "I'm sorry. I don't quite understand" his voice trailed off, his heart beating fast within his chest.

"Can we talk, Mr. Neely?" she asked gently.

"Talk? Oh, sure…yes, of course." He called to Paul to take over for a few minutes, then he led the girl to a quiet booth at the rear of the bar. They sat down, and Mac sat looking at her intently, finding it almost impossible to believe that this was not Kim seated across from him. How could any two people look so much alike?

She sat studying him for a moment, then she spoke. "I hope I haven't upset you, Mr. Neely, but I had to talk to you."

Mac, finally breaking out of his trance, replied, "Oh, no. Of course not, Miss…Miss Ching? Ah, can I order you a drink?"

"Oh, no thank you, Mr. Neely. I don't drink. A glass of ice water would be nice, though." Mac waved Joyce over and placed an order for ice water for the young woman and, feeling he needed something a little stronger, an Old Fashioned for himself.

Mac, when the drinks had been served, finally spoke. "Did I understand you to say you were Kai Ching's sister?" She nodded, and he went on. "You'll have to forgive me, but for a moment I thought you were…well, someone else…someone I…"

"Someone you loved very much," she finished for him. "I hope you won't feel I'm being too personal, but Mr. Lindham told me all about what happened…the fire and all. I'm very sorry."

"There's nothing for you to be sorry for. Life has a way of lifting one up only to dash him down hard just when he gets used to flying." Mac knew he had not been able to keep the bitterness he felt out of his voice.

"This isn't the first time I've run into a victim of my brother's cruelty. He was born evil! Even as a little boy, he did horrible things. He was terribly cruel to any animals that got in his path, and he loved to play hurtful, spiteful games with other people's lives. It seems like I'll never be completely free of him even now that he's dead."

"Dead?" Mac breathed.

"Yes. He died in the prison hospital two days ago. They thought he was recovered enough to be taken to jail, but there was some internal bleeding they hadn't caught. When they tried to move him... well...I never saw him, but they tell me it was for the best, his face had been so badly burned that he was hideous to look at. He couldn't have lived with that, not with his bloated ego."

Mac sat there trying to digest what he was hearing. Kai dead. He knew he should have felt elated, but somehow, it didn't seem to matter. Kai's death didn't really change anything. And somehow it seemed like it was too easy a way out for a fiend like Kai.

"I never knew he had any relatives. I guess I thought he must have just hatched out of some primordial egg from prehistoric days. I just didn't picture him with a sister, a mother, and father."

"He didn't either," sighed Lian. "Our mother and I lived in Viet Nam, where Kai made his money supplying your GIs with drugs. Kai provided for us financially, our father having been killed by communist scouts near our village."

It seemed to make her feel better to talk, and Mac wanted to know about this quiet, lovely girl. "There was certainly no love lost between Kai and my mother and me," she continued. "But he did see to it that we had food and shelter. Women in Asia are not brought up to fend for themselves. It's a very poor country, and women without protection do not survive for very long, not decent women, anyway."

"When Kai began being successful with his 'business', he moved to Saigon and took us with him. We wondered about this seeming 'kindness' at the time, but put our doubts aside and tried to be grateful to him for his protection. He put me through the International School in Saigon, a thing rare for women."

"Mother never told me of her greatest fear. She knew Kai was by then also dealing in prostitutes, but she could do nothing to stop him. She never voiced it, but her biggest fear was for me. She did not want Kai involving me in his dirty dealings."

"When the war, or police action as it was laughingly called, was over, we couldn't stay in Saigon any longer. Kai left for the States, on the run, and left us to our own resources."

Mac listened attentively, wondering at the bravery of these two women, on their own in a war-torn country.

Lian continued, "We wandered around the outskirts of Saigon for a while, hiding in holes dug out of the ground, eating any kind of garbage we could get our hands on, Mother all the time frightened to death soldiers would find us and rape us. Finally, a friend of my father's managed to get us on a boat. Just one of the hundreds of small boats carrying what you people called 'the boat people'."

"Once on the boat, it seemed like my mother just gave up. She was never the same after that. She blamed herself for our plight. She sat in the boat, moaning and praying to Buddha for hours, to forgive her the sin of bringing a devil into the world. Her fever got progressively worse."

"Had we had sufficient food or medical supplies, she might have survived, as it was, we buried her at sea, along with 3/4th of the people who had left the shore with us."

"What was left of our little band were picked up three days later by an American rescue ship, which brought me to your Island of New York. A week later, having survived all the paperwork at customs, I found myself among a group that were to be allowed to remain in the United States. We were sent to your state, Florida."

"But," Mac was thoroughly caught up in her story now, "How did you wind up in New York again?"

"When I found I was to be shipped to a type of refugee camp in this, Florida, I asked to speak to someone in authority in your government. I was finally allowed to speak to a man with your FB... FBI, I think?" Mac nodded, enthralled.

"I explained to him that I had a brother in the United States, and that I thought he was living in New York, the City." Mac loved her accent, which was much more pronounced than Kim's had been. "I told them I did not want to be sent to a camp, and that I felt if I could find my brother, he would be responsible for me. I was afraid Kai would force me into prostitution, but I decided to handle one problem at a time, and right then, I did not want to be in a camp with a bunch of strangers. I didn't feel my virtue would last too long there, either, and figured if I had to sell my body, it would be better in a clean bed with satin sheets." She looked keenly at Mac. "Does that shock you, Mr. Neely?"

"I'm afraid nothing shocks me much anymore, Miss Ching. Please go on," Mac urged.

"They changed my orders to read New York, and let me join another smaller group of refugees who had relatives in that city."

Mac couldn't help staring at her. As she talked, all he could see was Kim. The same expressions, the same lilt to the voice, the same softly slanted almond-shaped eyes. "Oh, forgive me, Miss Ching. I know I shouldn't stare, but you look so much like…." He couldn't bring himself to say her name aloud yet. "It's just uncanny!"

"Not really. You see, my dear brother used me as a model for his original android known as Kim." She stopped as she noted the look of pain in his eyes. "Oh, please forgive me, Mr. Neely. Agent Lindham told me of what happened to you. I know this must be very difficult for you, a delicate subject to discuss."

Mac realized that she knew of his love for Kim, and that Kim had been an…. No damn it. She was human. As human as anyone he had ever known—no matter what they said. In his heart, he knew that Kim had somehow transcended her state of creation. Some miracle had brought her to life. She had loved, and in that love had become human, for what else made people "human" if not their capacity to love. She had loved him, and he her—and that was enough for him.

He forced his mind back to the present. "No, Miss Ching, it's good for me to talk about it. I haven't spoken to anyone about it since the fire. There was no one I felt would understand." Her eyes, holding shadows of her own painful life, told him that she would. "I know you'll agree with me that we just can't turn our backs on what is painful. Pain and loss are a part of everyone's life, unfortunately." His handsome, stubborn Irish chin came up. "I'm not ashamed of loving

Kim, and I'll never fully be able to forget her, but I'm still alive and like you, I am a survivor."

She ventured a shy smile, the first since she had spoken to him at the bar. She was truly beautiful when she smiled. She had class and dignity, a certain quality all her own. She had managed, now that Mac took time to look at her better, to make her Ward's basement dress look like a Saks 5th Avenue design. She was too thin, but her proportions promised a striking figure when she put on some weight. She was speaking earnestly.

"You are a very brave man, Mr. Neely. Mr. Lindham told me about what you did. How you fought Kai and Kato combined, all the efforts you and Kim made to bring his rotten business down around their heads." She smiled wryly, "I'm told Kai repented his actions just before he died. Gave the FBI a list of his compatriots. Funny, I would have sworn he didn't have a conscience."

"If I knew him at all, I'd guess he just wanted to see the others suffer with him. That's one guy I'm glad to see permanently out of action… the Bas…! Sorry."

"You can't call him anything I haven't already called him. Every time I think about him my skin literally crawls. To think a man could try to force his own sister into prostitution, then when he didn't succeed, model an…another woman…after her and try to force her into the same miserable life. Sometimes I think he used her to punish me. He was always jealous of me because mother loved me. She would have loved him, too, but he made that impossible. Oh, how I hated that man. I hated him then, and I hate him even more now." She cried, the hurt and anger surfacing, giving her beautiful face a depth that Kim's had never had.

He reached out tentatively and touched her hand. She looked up into his eyes and he could see the beginnings of trust. She relaxed a little.

"What is sad is that if all that evil genius could have been channeled into constructive projects, he could have been one of the great men of our day." Mac pondered. "What makes people choose the path to Hell on earth? Where along the way, do they get lost?"

"He was lost from the beginning. But what I don't understand is why he used me as a model, other than to laugh at me… and he didn't even know if I was still alive… probably thought I wouldn't survive. Maybe that's why he used me." It seemed to just occur to her. "I thought he would have used one of his beautiful girlfriends as a model, but they were alive, and maybe he figured I was dead. What a mind."

"Well, we can thank God that he is out of action. But what made you come here, Miss Ching?"

"Please call me Lian." She breathed a long sigh. "When Lt. Lindham told me about you, I decided to look you up. You see, you have become to me like a link between past and future. You knew my brother. And besides, I had nowhere else to go… no one to turn to. I thought that if we could just keep in touch… talk now and then, it wouldn't be so…so lonely." The last word came out very softly and hesitantly, as if she was too proud to admit her aloneness.

As Mac listened, he tried to pull himself together. It was just too uncanny…unbelievable! But here it was… happening. This beautiful, young girl before him was real. Like a dream or a prayer come true. Not Kim, of course, but so like her it made his head spin. He looked at her, his eyes and spirits filled with the truth of her. Her voice, so soft, like Kim's, the hair that if, let down from the braids, would be, he was certain, down to her waist. All her features were Kim's, or actually all Kim's features were Lian's. She was a living, breathing duplication of his love.

However, as he studied her more closely, he discerned that there were minute differences. This girl had some fine lines at the corners of her eyes, and the shadows beneath them told of little sleep and much anxiety. She was, as he had noted earlier, thinner than Kim, and she looked tired and lost and so very, very human that it touched his heart.

She had continued to talk during his inspection. "So, Inspector Lindham thought you might be able to suggest a place I could live until I got a work visa and could get a job," she finished.

Mac saw that she was at the end of her rope, and that it cost her a great deal to ask for any assistance. She was trying to be brave and worldly, but a tear escaped the corner of her eye and trickled down her cheek.

"Please forgive my imposing on you like this, a total stranger, but I know no one else in this country. I don't want to be a burden to anyone, but I have nowhere else to go to...no one." She put her hands over her face and wept quietly.

Mac leaned across the table and gently pulled her hands away from her face. He held the two small hands clasped gently between his own large ones. He spoke softly, as to a child. "Don't worry, you could never be a burden to me. It will make me the happiest man in the world to be able to help you in any way I can." She smiled at him through her tears, and his heart skipped a beat. What was it about beautiful, helpless women that made him feel so strong, so worthwhile?

"There's usually an empty room in my apartment house. We'll get you a room there until we can get you something nicer."

Tears welled up in her eyes again, but this time they were tears of gratitude and happiness. "Oh, thank you, Mr. Neely. Thank you so very much."

"There's one condition though, young lady," he smiled.

"What is that? I'll do anything...well...," she blushed.

He laughed for the first time since the fire, and it felt good. "The condition is that you stop calling me 'Mr. Neely.' I'm Mac to my friends. And we are going to be good friends, aren't we?"

She smiled. He continued. "And we will find some work here at the bar for you, off the record, of course, till your visa comes through. Do you think you could learn to help; Joyce serves drinks? It isn't very glamorous, but it's easy. Joyce would show you and she's a super gal. You'll like her."

"Oh, Mr. Neely...Mac...how can I ever thank you?" She smiled fully for the first time, and it was as if a light went on inside her. His heart did that funny flip-flop again.

He looked at her, and silently he thanked God for this second chance. He knew that as close as the resemblance, she wasn't Kim. She was her own person, with her own individuality. She might never learn to care for him, or respond as Kim had—maybe never with so profound a passion—but who could tell what the future might hold?

In the meantime, he would be her friend. He would be gentle with her; he would teach her to trust again.

It might take time, lots of it, but he was in no hurry. He would have her near him, and someday, perhaps...who knows, the good Lord might just bless their lives with love. Until then...he was willing to wait.

As he sat there holding her hands, she smiled up trustingly at him. Her hands were warm in his.

Whatever happened...he was alive again. Truly alive...and it felt great!!

The End

www.ingramcontent.com/pod-product-compliance
Lightning Source LLC
LaVergne TN
LVHW011713060526
838200LV00051B/2887